A
WASP FOR
A FIG

NATALIE PINTER

Natalie Pinter is the author of *The Fragile Keepers*. She has lived in various places around the United States and currently resides in Florida with her husband and son.

Praise for
A Wasp For A Fig

"Brimming with folky fever-dream imagery, A Wasp for a Fig reads like a modernized blend of Arthur Machen and Angela Carter."
— **C.F. Page,** Author of *Native Fear*

"A Dionysian feast of folk horror with a fast-paced, classically-inflected spin on the genre touchstones. A Wasp for a Fig is a garden of unearthly delights and horrors, where you'll find a strange and all-consuming darkness at the heart of paradise. You'll devour this book!"
— **Brian Asman,** Author of *Man, F*ck this House*

"Natalie Pinter is a wonderful storyteller. She does more than just write-she casts a cozy, tactile, and entrancing spell, which you become compelled to follow wherever it takes you."
— **Eric Shapiro,** author of *It's Only Temporary* & *Days of Allison*

A WASP FOR A FIG

Natalie Pinter

Close To The Bone Publishing

Close To The Bone
an imprint of Gritfiction Ltd
Northampton
Northamptonshire
NN4
www.close2thebone.co.uk

First published in Great Britain in 2025 by Close To The Bone

ISBN 979-8-89965-782-5

First Printing, 2025

for Cory

Forbidden Fruit a flavor has
That lawful Orchards mocks—
How luscious lies within the Pod
The Pea that Duty locks—

— Emily Dickinson

1

"That's my water," says Vishal.

Sylas swallows and frowns at the plastic bottle in his hand. "My bad. They were both sitting there."

"Yours was half-empty. Mine was full." Their gazes meet in the rearview mirror for an uncomfortable moment, then Sylas blinks slowly back at the road. "Got it. Apologies."

Vishal looks back down at his phone. "Never mind. Sorry." It's one of the good things about him. Vishal knows when he's being peevish.

Sylas glances at David in the passenger seat. David has rolled down the window and the wind tousles back his shaggy blond hair. Just now he looks like an overgrown child, chewing on the thumbnail of his right hand, and clutching the stuffed little bunny in his left. He wears the same punch-drunk expression he's been wearing for the last few hours.

For the last year.

There is a stretch of silence save for the barely audible music. They've listened to podcasts on obscure medical mysteries and string theory, a stand-up comedy album, then music—ambient hip-hop and Avant-pop, now, acid jazz. The three roommates have some overlapping tastes, fortunately, but nothing is hitting the mark anymore.

Sylas takes in the southeastern landscape through the windshield. The open sky. Puffy clouds, scudding against the pale blue. The road is flanked on either side by thin walls of dingy-looking scrub pine. Earlier, there were trailer parks between rundown gas stations and billboards informing them they were in the depths of the Bible Belt. Now, there is nothing.

Today is June 21st –the anniversary. They've set out from a campus in the northeast, leaving behind two other roommates—a pair of studious twin brothers from further north—who keep to themselves.

Their initial enthusiasm (or at least chivalrous motivation) has worn off as the hours have rolled by. They left just after 3 a.m. It was important to David to come. He'd not wanted to trouble Sylas and Vishal though. "You guys don't have to make the trek, seriously. I appreciate it, but I can't ask you to do that."

But Sylas and Vishal wouldn't hear of it. David shouldn't be alone for this. And they'd gotten almost excited at the prospect. *Let's drive all night!* An energy-drink-fused notion, the effects of which have long ago subsided. But they are compelled by David's desperation. Relieved to be able to do *something*. A gesture. Maybe it would help David turn a corner. Find some closure, however inadequate. Maybe it would help him sleep. They're in David's car and he's driven the lion's share of the journey. Sylas took over when he kept drifting toward the median. In the few hours since, David still has not slept.

David rolls down the window and Sylas smells something fresh and sweet. Something that beckons him. He slows the car and pulls over to the side of the road where it hasn't looked any different in any direction for miles. "Sylas?" David says his name softly. "Why are you stopping?"

"I thought we needed to get to—" Vishal is saying, but Sylas cuts him off. "Do you smell that?" Sylas gets out and slams the door.

"Smell what?" Asks Vishal. "Is this the place? I thought it was a little further."

"I smell it—wow," says David. It's a relief to stretch their legs. They walk through a swath of long grass. *Probably rife with ticks*—thinks Sylas. The grass is still wet from recent rain and makes little dark slashes at the ankles of his jeans. It's probably the early afternoon, but Sylas hasn't been paying attention to the time. The only sound is their footsteps on the squelchy ground. Clouds of midges swim in the hot, muggy air.

Vishal sneezes and rubs the bridge of his nose. His eyes are watery behind his foggy glasses. "I think I've got allergies here."

The pines ahead are shielding a denser woodland beyond. Sylas has never smelled something like whatever he's smelling now. It's wonderful. Perhaps it comes from some plant that only grows in this part of the country.

David catches up to Sylas and then ambles ahead of him and Vishal with the same leisurely-but-swift stride he's had since middle school. Even though this might not be the exact right spot, Sylas hopes it might be close enough for some symbolic act, some rite of mourning. Maybe David will tuck the rabbit at the foot of a tree and say some words. They need to get back home. Sylas has to work. So does Vishal. Sylas smacks his arm where a mosquito nips him. "I'm kinda ready for this to be over," he admits quietly to Vishal, wincing internally at his own lack of reverence. And yet his feet keep taking him forward, toward the smell.

He feels a little better when, after a pause, Vishal says, "Yeah, me too."

Awful as it is, the Fairchild family tragedy is starting to be assimilated into their new normal.

Merit is never coming back.

"We're doing the right thing though," Vishal says. "It's good he's got us around, especially you."

Just don't say we're like brothers, Sylas thinks.

Sylas and David have been inseparable since divine wisdom from their 7th grade science teacher assigned the two lone wolves to partner on a phototropism project. Sylas had sat down mutely next to a lanky boy with a faint lisp and a fondness for doodling at the edges of his papers. "Do you want to come over to my place tomorrow?" David had asked him. He had the palest blue eyes Sylas had ever seen. Sylas had arrived at the mansion, dazzled and self-conscious. But David didn't notice things like Sylas's unwashed clothes and had been nonplussed the first time he saw Sylas's aunt's cluttered trailer. But it was a mutually tacit decision that they were better off working at David's.

Up to that point, Sylas had had a few acquaintances at school, but nothing more.

Except for Ronan.

Sylas had met the boy when he was eight, and for once, living in a decent apartment. His mother had made it a long stretch before she imploded again, and Sylas was sent to live with Aunt Tracy. His aunt was his primary guardian for most of his childhood, but he'd had a few stints with his paternal grandmother too. He'd been shuffled back-and-forth, narrowly avoiding a life in foster care.

But that time, for almost a year, he'd been with his mom. They'd had a clean driveway and a tiny yard with a crab apple tree. It was the summer before third grade. Ronan was a year older. He was skilled on a skateboard and used part of his ample allowance to buy them both ice cream when the ice cream truck came around.

One hot day, they walked to the neighbourhood pool, an exciting and frightening place; with its smell of chlorine and coconut sunscreen, crowded with glamorous teenagers splashing and sunbathing.

Ronan had walked out onto the end of the diving board. "I want to show you something, c'mere."

"What?"

"C'mere, you can only see it if you look directly down." Ronan projected his voice loud enough for others to hear and Sylas imagined his people scenting his fear like sharks.

He took off his flip flops and stepped slowly onto the edge of the diving board, hands out to steady himself as he felt its springy jounce. Standing close to Ronan, Sylas noticed the sprinkling of freckles on the boy's nose. The little glints of gold in his green eyes. Ronan smiled as he pointed down to the water and said, "look!" Sylas peered over the edge and—in retrospect, predictably— Ronan shoved him in.

Sylas had gurgled and pawed at the water in panic for a few seconds before he started to sink and felt whooshing in his ears, a burning in his sinuses. A blinding panic. He didn't remember much but the aftermath: Light, and darkness. Frantic voices, dissolved in water. One EMT patting his back while another hooked him to an IV. The terrible burning in his chest and the smell of his own vomit. He didn't know how to swim. He didn't even own a bathing suit. Over time, he would try to believe it had just been a prank gone wrong, but something in the other boy's face on the diving board told him it was more sinister than that.

It wasn't until 7th grade that he found a kindred spirit in David. David, with his long, graceful neck usually sheathed in a turtleneck. David, with his gangly legs and languid gait that didn't serve him well in P.E. They were awkward together. Leery of other kids. Both were Honor students, dreamy, and possessed of an almost metaphysical wanderlust. The winter of that first year he'd stayed at the Fairchild's for Christmas; they'd spent hours worldbuilding planets of strange monsters and mountains of hematite in an online sandbox videogame. High school found them in many overlapping classes and Sylas helped David study when he got too distracted. The Fairchild home became Sylas's residence. He was no extra burden. They had a cook and a house cleaner. David's parents were conveniently elusive, preoccupied, and generous.

It was only at extended family gatherings that Sylas felt uncomfortable. One summer day, a cousin, a weaselly boy a few years older, told him, "It's easy to be generous when you're in the one percent." He nodded to the figures in the pool. (Sylas was sixteen then, a competent swimmer. To his aunt's credit, he'd gotten swim classes at the local Y after the pool fiasco and bodies of water had ceased to be wide wet maws waiting to enact violence upon him.) "Don't think you're one of them." Just a month after that conversation, the Fairchilds paid for Sylas and David to get their scuba diving certifications. But Sylas didn't go on the trip to Fiji. That trip was family only. And in their 2-week absence, the cousin's words, replayed in his mind over and over. *"Don't think you're one of them."*

David was not the only one Sylas had an affinity for. At first, Merit had been a quiet child in braids. Then, a moody, coltish pre-teen, with shadows beneath large eyes, not the pale blue of David's, but the grey color of a stormy sea. She spent most of her time in her room, listening to music. Later, when Sylas and David went to the same university—Sylas riding on scholarships—he saw Merit on summer break, swimming in the pool, having blossomed in high school with a couple of friends.

Winter break of their sophomore year they'd found a new version of Merit. She was dressed in black, with chrome nail polish and a nose ring; her hair, chopped to the scalp. She'd said to him, "Hey stranger," and hugged Sylas with unexpected affection. She had smelled like Bergamot and Earl Grey tea. Later, she'd joined them for a beer and a viewing of an arthouse film. After that, he'd only seen pictures online. She'd grown the hair out, dyed it maroon. Merit and David weren't particularly close, but they liked one another enough and shared inside jokes.

At the first call, a year ago, David wasn't too worried. Merit was nineteen by then. She'd been on her way to New Orleans to visit a friend—the first road trip by herself. But she'd never arrived at her friend's place. The next day, when no one could reach her on her cell, they still didn't panic. But as hours passed, and then another day went by with no phone calls or texts, David had started chain smoking a vape, constantly staring at the phone, texting family and friends. Within a week, there were news interviews, vigils, field cadaver dogs in this part of the southeast where her abandoned car had been found. The picture of her on the news and social media was a good one—with her wind-whipped hair faded fuchsia and brown. She wore a faint, hopeful smile. It was a picture to galvanize people to search, an image of an ill-fated youth to lament over.

There was no trace of her.

David had taken leave of school, but after months of dead-end leads, he'd resumed his courses, a gaunt, haunted-looking figure. Of course, his rent was paid. David was expected to work like everyone else, and he expected it of himself, but he didn't really *have* to. And his job at the museum was on hiatus partly due to the debilitating insomnia he'd developed over the last year.

The day before, David had approached Sylas and Vishal, eyes bloodshot, expression far away, "I need to go where she last was. I need to give her Tucker." He'd held up Merit's threadbare bunny which had lived on her bed through childhood and beyond.

2

"I wouldn't expect to see birches here," says Vishal. He takes off his flannel and ties it around his waist to reveal a shirt that reads, "Thermodynamics Is the Bacon of Science." He sneezes again. "How far does this go?" he asks. Over the next few minutes there are more rhetorical questions from Vishal about a highway they should be seeing, but Sylas had been spaced out behind the wheel for the last hour while Vishal navigated. He's been doing that lately, piggybacking off David's ineptitude.

Sylas has come around on Vishal over the last couple of years. Initially, he'd been chilly toward the handsome, gregarious cryptology major David had brought back to their house after a lecture one evening. A couple of months later, when Vishal needed a new room due to a burst pipe at his student housing, Sylas worried he counterbalanced David's softness too well. But Vishal was straight, and cosmopolitan enough not to care that Sylas wasn't, and that David's tastes were hazy and mysterious.

Sylas had wanted to be David's rescuer but settled on being his refuge. Possessed by an authoritative solicitude, when Merit vanished, Vishal had stepped between David and the world in a way Sylas couldn't. He'd been a competent liaison between David and his professors, getting him extensions on assignments. He'd shamed away the nosy and voyeuristic students on campus. But what made Sylas fully thaw on Vishal was one little offhand remark he'd made during the early days of Merit's disappearance. They were at the Fairchild's home and a detective had asked if Sylas was family and Vishal had said, "For all intents and purposes."

Vishal halts again, looking around. The scraggly pines have given way to a denser woodland. Sylas inhales another waft of something sublime. "You smell that?" he asks Vishal again.

Vishal shakes his head. Then, visibly inhaling, says, "Maybe. Flowers?" He calls out to David, "Hey, can you hold up, please."

David pauses but only his head moves, swivelling on his neck almost eerily, so just his chiselled, aquiline profile appears to them. "Yeah?"

Sylas hesitates. If there is a sentimental rite David intends to make, Sylas doesn't want to hurry him. He knows they need to get going, but he also wants to keep walking toward the scent. "Are we—uh—are we going much further?"

David blinks slowly. "It smells so good," he says in lieu of answering the question, and continues walking on, into the next section of woodland.

Vishal slows and turns to glance behind them. He throws up his hands. "Okay, this doesn't make any sense. How did we come from there?" He points to where the car is no longer visible through the trees, then he pulls out his phone. "Of course," he mutters. "Your phone on you?" he asks Sylas, shoving it back into his pocket.

Sylas shakes his head. "I left it in the car."

"I'd like to know where we are."

"Southern Alabama?" Sylas ventures.

"No, I mean *exactly* where—" Vishal gestures at their surroundings.

Sylas looks around. A part of him sees that Vishal is right to be confused. The landscape isn't making sense. This woodland park seems endless. There was supposed to be another road by this point. He doesn't answer.

They pick up the pace. Striving to keep his voice gentle, Vishal calls out to David again, "So, what's the plan? Can you hold up here for a second?"

David turns, looking somehow both serene and near delirium. He's been living in that thin t-shirt, covering his willowy frame for days. Looking at him clutching Tucker, Sylas feels a familiar ache. He wants to wrap him in his arms. "I think we're close," David says. He closes his eyes and inhales deeply. "Sorry, not much further I don't think. What *is* it?" he asks Sylas, as if Sylas should know.

"I don't know. It's nice though." An understatement. The aroma is growing narcotically glorious. A sublime union of mysterious blossoms and earthy minerals, wrapped in a bouquet of indigo sunshine. And it demands to be discovered. Sylas wants to keep going. It's become a beautiful day. It's not even too hot anymore. From somewhere ahead, the sound of a flute floats through the trees. Sylas and Vishal exchange a glance.

"Do you think… " The words peter out because he almost asks, *Do you think it has something to do with Merit?*

Vishal's eyes suddenly go wide behind his glasses. "Wow. My allergies were bothering me, but I think I smell it now. What *is* that?"

This is when Sylas first feels a little, *red-light-of-alarm*. A throbbing glow somewhere inside his consciousness. *What are we doing? The car is still parked on the side of the road. Like Merit's car a year ago.*

Sylas places his hand on the trunk of a tree and tilts his head back. Spanish moss drips from the live oaks that seem anthropomorphic. He's put in mind of shawls on statuesque maidens. Other flora seems out of place in this southern landscape. "I know there's oaks and cypress around here, but these are huge," he says. "I wouldn't have expected to see evergreens like that. This is a straight up forest." He points ahead at some dark green towers that looked like they'd be more at home in the Pacific Northwest.

"Yeah, this is weird," Vishal agrees, taking in the baffling landscape. "And it's cooled off." Silvery flute music fades in and out from up ahead. "Is this a park? Like a state park?" he asks. "Maybe there's something going on. I didn't see it on the map."

They continue, and soon a creek appears on the left side of the path. "How long have we been walking?" Sylas asks suddenly.

"Five—ten minutes, maybe." says David.

"No way, Vishal huffs. "Longer than that, right?

The foliage flanking the path gradually gives way— not to the sporadic blush of yellow or pink wildflowers but to a botanical garden: roses, zinnias, tulips—and others as colorful as those painstakingly cultivated in the Fairchild's neighbourhood blanket the world around them.

Sylas can't help himself; the biology nerd in him is coming out. "Look at this! Amanita Muscaria." He points to a cluster of squat, bright red mushrooms covered in white dots. He steps a few feet away and leans over two dark pink flowers shaped like lozenges. "And these are pitcher plants. They're carnivorous."

As they continue, Sylas again feels the sporadic pin-prick of red-light. A little alarm crying, *"Where the hell are we?"*

The path curves gradually right, and a woman appears some twenty feet from them.

"The hell?" whispers Vishal.

She's dressed in a two-piece, saree-inspired, yellow confection. Her feet are sandaled, and her golden hair is ornately coiled, topped with a circlet of yellow flowers. Red-brown swirls and symbols wrap over her forearms and the back of her hands. She smiles, like she's amused and well-disposed to them. "Are you lost?" she asks as they approach.

Sylas stammers, "Well, maybe."

They are standing with ample space between themselves and the woman, vaguely sensing this is the right thing to do, being that she is alone in the presence of three strange men. Aside from the fanciful attire, there is something else that is odd about her, but before Sylas can decide what it is, she turns back the way she's come and calls over her shoulder, "Follow me instead." Without a word, they comply.

The red-light pulses dimly inside of Sylas. A small part of him is grappling with it: They entered a scraggly grove far beyond the side of the road. There should be the sprawl of asphalt, more dismal clusters of strip malls. Instead, they are following this unlikely creature through a lush, storybook wood. But before he can explore this concern any further, the scent smothers his anxiety.

Vishal walks up alongside the woman. "I'm Vishal, what's your name?" He offers his hand but she either ignores it or doesn't notice.

"Viola."

Sylas strides up and offers a little wave. "I'm Sylas."

David, a few feet behind them now, is oblivious to social graces as the flute music grows louder. After a moment, Vishal speaks for him. "And this is David."

"Oh, hey," David says softly.

"Is there a party going on or something?" Vishal asks her.

She glances back at him. "It's the solstice," she says.

"Oh yeah, that's right, I forgot it's the solstice," Vishal says. Then, "So, are you from around here?"

"Yes."

She slows to pluck a flower from the side of the path. On the back of her hand is a sort of tear-drop shaped symbol, slightly vulvic. "I like your henna," Sylas offers. He feels a trickle of sweat running down his back even though it's no longer hot outside.

"Thank you." She lifts the flower to her face and looks up at him. It hits Sylas what is strange about her appearance: her irises are a brilliant shade of lavender, and her eyes are strangely wide set. She's not unlovely, but she's odd looking. Puppet-like and fey. She drops the flower and continues along the path.

Vishal slows. "Wait, shouldn't we—what about the car?"

Suddenly Vishal's question annoys Sylas. He and David don't reply. Who cares about the car? For inexplicable reasons, finding the source of this scent has gained priority over other concerns. A few minutes later, Vishal tries again, whispering to them, "Do you think we should ask her about Merit? Maybe she knows something."

"I'm following his lead," Sylas says, with a nod toward David. *Has David been expecting to find this place? No, of course not.*

The flute's tempo quickens as the wood grows denser. Gnarled branches arch over their heads, dimming the path for a stretch. They walk faster through the tunnel of trees, to where bright sunlight beckons them beyond, and soon they emerge into another clearing. If the GPS they'd been following earlier was remotely accurate, what they see now defies the laws of physics.

In a sprawling meadow sits a stone palace, a roughly pyramidal construct of layered platforms spangled with flowers and vines spiralling down columns. Fountains flow into gleaming turquoise pools. It's the kind of architecture only seen in images of elusive travel destinations or films. It's the kind of place Sylas has daydreamed of throughout his life. And it reminds him of something else, too, an image he saw long ago, but he can't quite remember what it was.

On the verandas are women dressed like Viola in silky sarees or flowy dresses, and men, shirtless, or wearing vests, and billowy, harem-style pants. Others are nude, lounging around the pools, drinking from goblets and eating grapes in a cliché vision of wanton luxury.

Vishal removes his glasses, rubs the lenses, and puts them back on. "It's like… like—"

"The Hanging Gardens of Babylon," Sylas says, realizing what the structure reminds him of: A picture in one of the few books he had growing up, a richly illustrated book about the Seven Wonders of the World.

"Hah," Vishal says, "How in the hell… "

Blinking under the sunlight after the shade of the wood, they follow Viola across the meadow. The music dissolves as they ascend the first set of stairs amidst the sound of muffled laughter and murmuring. The people nudge one another and point. Some of them wave and smile. They all possess wide-set, lavender eyes.

"Where the hell are we?" Vishal blurts out. Before anyone replies to this, he asks David, "What—what about your car?"

Sylas wonders if it was hard for Vishal to push that question all the way through his mind and out of his mouth. The car feels so trivial, so far away.

Before David replies, Viola speaks. "If you leave now you cannot return. The path disappears when the sun goes down."

They look around. Somehow, it's already the early edge of dusk. Without speaking, they continue after her, up onto the widest of several grand verandas. After another set of steps, they reach a pair of large stone doors. Etched above the doors is the same vaguely teardrop shape that is painted in henna on the back of Viola's hand. This carving is clearer, more detailed. Curved lines, like half-moons and thirds-of-a-circle wind around a center where more lines suggest darkness: *a cavern, a ring, a hole, an entrance.* "Come, I'll take you to the nobility," Viola says.

Through the doors is a tiled room interspersed with pillars and tall vases of flowers. A fountain sits in the center. Behind, late afternoon sunlight spills down from a spacious courtyard that appears to lead back into the garden-wood. Two hallways, garlanded with a spiky, purple flower, branch to the right and left.

Sylas glances at David, who stares up at the ceiling at yet another carving of the ubiquitous symbol.

Viola guides them down the left hallway where they reach a coiled staircase which they ascend in single file. At the top of the stairs a wall on the right gives way to curtain of green vines which she pulls aside, crying, "I bring foundlings!" She waves for them to follow her out onto a balcony that looks down over the sprawling front of the palazzo they've just entered.

"Our nobility," Viola says.

Facing the balcony is a woman reclined on a papasan chair, and a man lying in a hammock. A sleepy-looking topless young woman fans them. They turn to their guests. "Foundlings," Viola says again, seeming pleased with herself. She gestures to each of them in turn and says their names.

The 'nobility' don't appear any different from the rest of the community. "Helio," says Viola, indicating the man. Helio wears a yellow toga and a crown of laurel leaves. In one hand, he clutches a goblet, and he waves at them with the other.

"And Vinca Minor," says Viola.

The woman stands up from the chair. She's tall, wasp-waisted, with ebony skin and gold rimming her wide, lavender eyes. She wears an apricot gown and a crown of white orchids. She slightly inclines her head. "Welcome."

Helio stirs from the hammock, sitting up clumsily. Clear liquid sloshes onto the stone steps. "You made it." He lifts his goblet in a toast.

"She led us here," says Sylas, looking at Viola.

"Well done," purrs Vinca Minor, smiling at Viola.

"Smelled something nice, eh?" Helio asks Sylas, waggling his eyebrows.

"We're actually parked off the side of the road," says Vishal. His forehead has a sheen of sweat, and his gaze is effortfully avoiding the bare breasts of the woman fanning the 'nobility.' "I'm not really sure how we ended up here."

Stop resisting, man. You're going to have a stroke trying to make this logical, Sylas thinks.

Helio smirks. "Of course. You wouldn't be. You *never* are." He points up at the sky. "It's the light at this time of the year. *Her* nectar is stronger. So folks"—he makes a fluttering gesture—"wander in."

Sylas glances at David who looks delirious, about to collapse. Sylas has a fleeting fantasy of catching him in his arms.

"Only three," Viola sighs. "We used to get more."

"The day is not over yet," says Helio brightly. "Remember last year?"

When Viola doesn't reply, David finally speaks. "What happened last year?"

"Are you expecting more or something?" asks Vishal, his question overlaps with David's.

Helio shrugs. "Couldn't say." It's unclear whose question he's answering.

There is a pause and Sylas shivers as the fog in his mind briefly lifts and the red-light color changes to red-violet. The color is still urgent, but different somehow. He sympathizes again with Vishal's incredulity. Gripping their mission in his mind, Sylas blurts: "We are actually here because of his sister," He looks at David and prompts him, whispering, *"Merit."*

David blinks a few times, then addresses the strangers. "Yeah, right. God, I'm so spaced out. So, my sister disappeared a year ago." Moving Tucker into his other hand, David reaches into the pocket of his jeans and pulls out his phone and taps at the dark screen a few times to no avail. It looks wrong in this place. Ugly and inert. With a sigh, he pockets it again. "I was going to show you a picture. Her name is Merit." He swallows. "She's nineteen—well, twenty now." He lifts his hand. "About this tall. Brown hair. Gray eyes? Her car was found around here—" he frowns "—sort of around here."

"Not familiar to me," Helio says, yawning widely. He looks to Vinca Minor and Viola. "Do you know of whom he speaks?"

Vinca Minor shakes her head. David steps over to the balcony and gazes down as if he's looking for Merit among the figures below.

Settling back into his hammock Helio chuckles to himself.

Vinca Minor says to Viola, "take our guests to their chamber so they can relax before the feast."

"Mmmm." Helio closes his eyes and lays back in the hammock. "Yes, they can relax. Why not? It's just the first night."

"Come. I'll take you to your chambers," Viola says.

"I need to look for Merit," says David softly, still gazing over the balcony.

Vinca Minor steps toward him and says tenderly, "Why don't you rest first?" Her voice is soothing, velvety.

There are dark circles beneath David's eyes and his eyelids now have a hooded, fatigued droop. He rubs his forehead. "Yeah, okay. I—I can't think straight right now."

They retreat through the vines and Viola leads them down the hall to another door. "Here," she says, as they enter a large room with a bathing pool flanked by low-to-the-floor pallet-beds. Against the far wall is a broad, open window. Underneath it is a table with a pitcher and goblets, fruit, cheese, nuts. "After you're clean and rested you can dress for our party tonight." Viola opens a wardrobe and pulls out clothing which she lays on one of the pallets. Then she steps to the door. "I will return to check on you soon."

"Thank you," says Vishal. "But we'd really like if you could just tell us—"

But she slips from the room and closes the door before he finishes.

There is a beat of silence. *What if it's an elaborate prank?* Sylas thinks. *A reality series with a massive budget.* But no, all the absurdity is authentic somehow. Dream logic or no, this place feels lived in. It has a history, and the scent still needs accounting for.

Finally, Vishal says, "Well, this is unexpected. Who knew the southeast harbored something this bougie." He claps his hands together. "So, what do you guys think? My guess is one of two things: either our bottled water was spiked with something strong, or we're dead and this is the afterlife." He shoots a nervous smile at Sylas. "Did you plow into an oncoming truck or something?"

"Not that I'm aware of," Sylas whispers. Then he asks David, "You're not—" He clears his throat, struggling to form the words. "—worried about leaving your car?" He understands now why Vishal wants to cling to the car. It feels safe. Real. A big machine. A heavy anchor to a world that makes sense. Maybe Vishal is right, and it shouldn't be abandoned.

But David shakes his head. "Not really, Sylas." Something about the way David says his name brings the gravitas of the situation to the forefront. Their eyes meet for a moment. Then he says, "Look, I'm too delirious to figure this out right now." David strips off his clothes and climbs into the pool. Sylas's heart flutters and he looks away. "What?" David says, at Vishal's startled expression. He lowers himself into the steaming pool with a groan. "When in Rome, right?"

Vishal goes to the window and looks down over the front side of the palazzo. Laughter and flute music drift up to them.

It occurs to Sylas that they haven't found the source of the sublime scent, but he doesn't want to bring it up just now. "How's the temperature?" he asks David.

"Perfect." David bobs his head under and comes up slicking his hair back from his face. "Really perfect." David points at the rendering of the tear-drop shaped oval lines carved above the window. "I wonder what that means. It's everywhere." Sylas knows David is going to become preoccupied with this particular mystery. He's an art history scholar with a penchant for peculiar iconography.

Vishal tilts his head back to look at it. "We should ask them what it means. We should ask them a lot of questions, actually. So, the police searched all over this area and never came to this place?"

Sylas frowns, rubbing his temples. Part of him agrees completely. *He's right to have questions. This is all crazy. We need to get back.* At the same time, he wishes Vishal would shut up.

"You know they didn't," David replies.

"Did *you* know this was here?" Vishal asks him pointedly.

Punch drunk with fatigue, David still manages to look incredulous. "Of course not."

"Then," Vishal lets the word hang.

David swishes his arms back and forth in the pool, his bloodshot eyes fixed on the symbol. "I've thought of so many scenarios, you know? There are the horrible, obvious possibilities, like she was raped and butchered. There are pieces of her in a ditch somewhere. Or she's trapped in a psycho's cellar. But sometimes I wonder if she was abducted by aliens. Or joined a circus. Or a cult. So, in a way this almost feels as impossible as the rest." It's the most David has spoken about Merit in a long time.

"Do you think she was here?" Vishal asks softly.

"Maybe," David says, "It feels like there's answers here. One way or another." David heaves himself out of the pool, shakes his head, spraying droplets. He reaches for one of the towels folded neatly on the edge of the tub. He asks Sylas, "Why did you ask me to pull over when you did?"

"The smell," Sylas says softly. He shrugs. "I got a whiff of it when you rolled down the window."

David looks at him with an unreadable expression and then picks up his dirty clothes. He wrinkles his nose. Then he looks at the garments Viola laid out for them and begins to change into the harem pants and light vest. "Vishal, you're going to look like Aladdin."

"I'm not wearing that crap," Vishal mutters.

"It's nice," David says, running his fingers along vest. "Soft." He sways a little. "I'm sorry guys, but—," he flops face down onto one of the pallets—muffled, he says, "—But I'm just going to shut my eyes for a bit here."

After a minute Sylas shrugs and strips and climbs into the pool. After bathing, he finds his old clothes fusty just as David did. He too dons the harem pants and vest. The fabric feels odd but pleasing, like a texture between silk and leather. Vishal takes a quick dip and then puts his own clothes back on, but after a few minutes of sighing and fidgeting, he too changes into the harem pants and foregoes anything on top.

It's been hours since they've eaten. The dried fruit is plump and tasty, the nuts are savory. Sylas pours a glass of water from the pitcher. It tastes crisp and not quite carbonated, but pleasantly spicy somehow. After snacking, Sylas and Vishal each sit on one of the other pallets. David has rolled over and is sleeping on his back. Sylas watches the soft rise and fall of his chest.

"Did you notice their eyes?" Vishal asks him quietly.

"Yeah."

"Are they even people?"

"I don't know. They're like, nymphs or something?"

Through the window, the sky is turning gray.

Sylas closes his eyes and sees David in the pool, waist deep and sparkling wet. A tiny puddle of water droplets on his clavicle. His sharp jaw and thinly sculpted biceps. A memory surfaces: the memory that haunts and tantalizes. They were seventeen. Summer before senior year. Drunk for the first time on Schnapps, they had been laughing hysterically at something. David had tucked his hair behind his ear, and they'd kissed. It was like a light Sylas had never known existed inside of himself was switched on. The softness of David's lips opened to a shining warmth he wanted to fall into.

And then David had pulled away, laughing nervously. Or terrified. "What are we doing?"

The ground had opened up under Sylas. *Who had started it?* He didn't know. "I—I'm sorry." Something indeterminable had flickered over David's face. Contempt, or fear, or anxiety. Something painful. Sylas had backed away, tucking or untucking his shirt, suddenly sweaty. He'd gone to another room.

In the days that followed, David had not been unkind, but he'd been formal, politely distant. Finally, Sylas called his aunt was scooped up in under an hour. He'd lain in the small extra bedroom with the blinds shut and floundered in an abyss of suicidal ideation for three days. Then David had shown up on the porch in a hooded sweatshirt in the summer heat; eyes red, wondering at his abandonment. "Why did you leave? You don't have to go away."

Sylas returned to his room at the Fairchilds. It was never discussed. They forged their way through a few weeks of awkwardness, pretending everything was normal, until one day, before fall, it actually was.

In school, David had been more interested in his courses than anything else. His desk was littered with printed images of hieroglyphs and library books on Mayan pottery. His sophomore year, he'd dated a girl, Nadja. But after a few months it dissolved into a lagging friendship.

Sylas had a few flings. He spent almost six months in a relationship with a very nice, very dull guy, ten years his senior named Jeremiah. But Sylas was always preoccupied by daydreams of David. He imagined them living in New England villas. On a houseboat. In a penthouse overlooking some sparkling European city. Some fantastical alternate dimension where Sylas's wealth had grown equal to the Fairchilds. In his fantasies, his success was never achieved through adjacent nepotism. He received a Nobel prize in physics, he turned out to be the long-lost heir of some minor royalty. Hell, he won the lottery.

There is a knock. "Yes? Come in," says Vishal, sitting up.

Viola opens the door. "I will show you some of the Garden before it gets dark." They follow her gaze to the window where soft yellow light of dusk serves as a blanket for a few strangely large and pink-ish stars.

It's decided that David is best left to sleep. As they follow Viola, they glimpse figures mingling in open doorways, leaning against the balustrades that line every story. The palace is shaped like a narrow crescent moon, wrapping halfway around a seemingly endless woodland. At the end of the hall is a wide staircase, curving to the ground and depositing them onto a patio. One half of the sky is now covered in a wrinkled swath of dark clouds encroaching the expanse.

Ahead is a pleached alley—a long rounded passage of greenery, but Viola leads them left of this, along shimmery tiled pathways flanked by flower beds and walls of hedges. Vishal clears his throat. "Where are we exactly?"

"Sepal Estra."

Vishal repeats the name to himself then asks, "So you're all residents?" he asks. "Is it a co-op?"

"Yes, we live here." She smiles in a way that put Sylas in mind of someone indulging the curiosity of a child.

The flower beds give way to fruit trees being harvested by the nymphs. Viola strides down rows of fruit trees: figs, berries, apricots, apples, lemons, pears. The wheelbarrows are full, and most of the trees, picked clean.

"Hail, Papaver," Viola says to a strapping nymph. She gestures to them and says, "Vishal and Sylas. Two of our foundlings." The twee descriptor is starting to chafe.

"Welcome." The nymph bobs his head at them. Then to Viola he says mildly, "I told you there'd be some."

When he lifts the wheelbarrow's handles to move on, Vishal steps in front of it. "Hey, we know someone who may have come by this way. Do you remember seeing a new girl come around here about a year ago? Brown hair and blue eyes?"

"Gray," Sylas corrects him softly.

"No," Papaver says, then spares a glance at Viola.

Vishal studies him for a moment. "That's too bad. I would think you'd remember someone who had eyes that weren't purple."

Papaver doesn't reply but meets Vishal's gaze steadily.

"C'mon, man, give it up for now," Sylas mutters, under his breath. Just observing this awkward exchange is strangely enervating, and it's clear the nymphs aren't forthcoming.

After a moment, Papaver maneuvers the wheelbarrow around them and wheels the fruit away.

"You must have a taste," Viola says to them.

They eat luscious cherries and plums. Their tongues are tantalized by new tannins as they try a plump citrusy thing like the hybrid of a lime and a green grape. And from a small, willow-like tree, they taste tiny orange berries with sweet, jammy juice.

They move on, passing an herb garden where nymphs harvest fragrant green shrubbery, and then cross through a break in a hedge.

Something compels Sylas to hold his breath, pressing down the hypnotic scent. After several seconds, the red-violet light rises from the depths and pulses so hard, awareness and panic tear through, clawing at the thin, fleshy walls of Sylas's mind. It's a war inside of him. He stops in his tracks, fists clenched. "We need to get back home." *Yes, home. But… why, really?* "What—what are we doing here?" Sylas forces the words out.

He takes a breath, and the red-violet light is snuffed out. More than ever, Sylas has the urge to forsake all concerns. To drop the burden of trying to make sense of this. He looks up to see creamy white blossoms as they pass beneath a magnolia tree. What if they could stay here in this paradise where David's fortune and Sylas's penury doesn't matter? *Sepal Estra.*

"Our goddess, Nepenthe, has brought you," Viola says. "She is waking."

"Is she…—" Vishal flounders. "What do you mean?"

"Do not trouble yourself. You will understand soon." She turns and leads them along the cobbled path. *A goddess?* Images flood through Sylas's head. *A 50 foot tall glowing nymph. A pre-Raphaelite visage in the clouds.*

The air thickens. Clouds darken the shadows under the stately trees and small springs.

Vishal points at a dense green hedge to their right. "What is that?"

"The labyrinth," Viola says. She's about to say something else, when a dramatic rumble of thunder cuts her off. They feel the first kiss of rain as a nymph approaches them, eyes eager. "The nobility requests you return to the palace. More foundlings have arrived!"

They abandon the cobbled path and cut through the trees to the portico parallel to the garden, as the rain pours in earnest. Viola leads Sylas and Vishal back up the curving staircase. They quickly check on the still-sleeping David, then continue down the hall and pass through the vined curtain of the nobility's chamber.

A young man speaks to Helio and Vinca Minor in a thick twang. "And then I said to these two, 'Kansas and all that, right?'" He wears a baseball cap and is handsome in a ruddy, salt-of-the-earth way. Bluish-gray tattoo sleeves cover his arms and part of one hand. A girl leans, a little knock-kneed, against him. She wears a tank top and shorts. Her wet hair is in a loose bun. Another girl, with a pageboy haircut and a black swan tattoo on her shoulder, stares over the balcony watching the front palazzo getting watered. The new 'foundlings' are soaked, but the low, vaulted ceiling over the balcony shields them from the rain now. They look out of place to Sylas, disorienting.

Tony, Kat, and their friend, Zoe, had been walking along an underpass when they were drawn deeper into the wood by an alluring scent.

"Six," says Vinca Minor, smiling. "Nepenthe will be pleased."

3

The new foundling's chamber is linked to theirs by the small door that leads to a toilet area. Kat, Tony, and Zoe's room is similar, though their bathing pool is against the far wall rather than in the middle of the room. An image of the symbol directly over it reflects in in the still water. "I'm not going to say what that reminds me of," says Tony. Zoe rolls her eyes.

Sylas, Vishal, and Zoe retreat into their room while Kat and Tony bathe. "So, you guys aren't from around here?" Zoe asks.

In low voices, so as not to wake the sleeping David, Vishal and Sylas tell her of their trek from school, and when they get to the reason for it, Zoe whispers, "No way! That's Merit Fairchild's brother? We were just talking about her disappearance the other day, before we found this place. It was a big deal around here. My uncle helped with one of the first search parties." They are all quiet for a moment. "I'm not sure why I'm not more freaked out," she says eventually. "I don't understand where we are."

"Me neither," says Vishal. He glances at Sylas and addresses him. "You're taking it all pretty well."

Sylas frowns, realizing he can't think of a way to articulate the red-violet light. After a moment he says, "Sometimes I feel this wave of, what-the-fuck, and then something stops my mind from going into a full-blown panic."

Zoe is nodding. "I know what you mean. It has something to do with the smell. I'm too calm." Her eyes drift over to David. "Poor guy," she says. "No one here has been able to tell you guys anything about Merit? No one has heard of her?"

"No," Vishal says. "We've been asking."

"I guess that's not surprising," she says softly. "This place feels out of time."

Sylas drifts over to the window again while Zoe and Vishal converse in whispers. Beyond the palace lays the meadow and then the woods—the forest really. They could be in another country altogether. In another world.

When Kat and Tony appear, dressed in fresh nymph clothing, Sylas and Vishal fill them in on David and their circumstances while Zoe takes a turn in the bath. She emerges a short time later wearing a powder blue gown. Kat whispers something to her and they laugh and spin in a circle. They do a little improv dance routine before breaking into laughter that finally wakes up David.

4

"To our beloved, Nepenthe!" Helio lifts his crystal goblet; it glints in the light of the tall candles along the table.

"Nepenthe!" rejoins the crowd. Their voices have a distinct, songbird quality, Sylas has noticed. It's twilight. Most of the nymphs now wear face paint or masks in a style reminiscent of the Green Man. Though rather than leaves, the faces are formed of petals.

The rain ceased some time ago, abruptly as a faucet turned off. Water from puddles and shrubbery evaporates in the balmy air releasing scents of jasmine and honeysuckle. Lying underneath is the Scent. Music plays in the distance.

"To the Holy Hunger!" calls Vinca Minor, raising her glass.

"The Holy Hunger!" echoes the crowd. Candles gild an opulent charcuterie along the rows of tables: a cornucopia of fruit, pots of honey, wedges of cheese. Berries gleam like jewels next to glasses filled with clear, sweet and spicy "nectar." After just half a glass, Sylas feels euphoric.

"What's special about today?" asks Kat.

"Such a question," sneers a nymph sitting a few seats down. "They are always so superior to their soil and stars. Them and their small flowers."

Kat drops her gaze, looking troubled.

Zoe ventures, "It's the solstice?"

"In your world, yes," Viola says. "*Here,* it is more than that."

David leans over and whispers to Kat, "Don't feel bad, I didn't realize it was the solstice either." She shoots him a quick, grateful smile. Then she taps Tucker, the stuffed rabbit, who sits to the right of David's place like a pet. "Careful he doesn't get messy," she says.

Tony bites into a pear. "This is so good."

"There is no banquet tomorrow." a nymph tells him. "Only nusha."

"Nusha!" the nymphs cry excitedly, some of them pounding the tabletop.

Next to Sylas, Vishal is struggling again and it's almost physically palpable. "Is it some sort of flower cult?" he whispers anxiously.

"Would it be worse than all the fire and brimstone shit we saw on the billboards earlier?" Sylas mutters.

"So, what do you do around here?" Tony asks a nymph with a mask covering the upper half of her face.

"What everyone does. I pluck the bounty and make merry," she replies, as if it's obvious.

A procession of masked dancers emerges from the pleached alley, arms undulating while two of them hold up a banner with the symbol. Three of them clutch giant flowers by the stems and twirl them in unison. The blossoms are the circumference of beach balls.

"Them and their small flowers."

Sylas winces as the red-violet light begins to softly glow from the murky depths of his consciousness. The color is changing, becoming more violet. He takes a deep breath and another sip of nectar, and after a few seconds, the light dissipates.

"Are those real?" Vishal asks, staring at the impossibly enormous blossoms.

Not tearing her gaze from the dancers, Viola says, "Where do you think your raiment comes from?"

They look down and touch their clothing. Before they can remark on this, dancers sashay over to the tables as Viola rises from her seat and says, "The foundlings should return to the palace." But the music drowns out her voice and masked dancers clasp the foundlings by their hands and draw them away from the banquet tables, leading the group down the dark green tunnel of the pleached alley and out into the parkland. They move under arbors and around trees, weaving their way past the herb garden from a different side.

As they enter a glade filled with more nymphs, the dance disperses. Light from bonfires and luminaries reveal musicians on a circular dais. It had seemed like there were dozens of nymphs when they'd first approached the palace, but now there must be hundreds. The crowd extends up into the tall trees, where bioluminescent ivy drips from the branches. Rope bridges connect platforms some thirty feet over their heads. The bridges converge at a sort of bullseye, a center point above something hidden behind a large wall of hedge.

When Sylas sees some of the nymphs have bows and arrows slung over their shoulders, the red-violet light flares again, briefly.

David nudges him and points to a colorful bed of absurdly big flowers. Amaryllis, like huge starbursts. Crocus, like goblets for a giant. Beyond the flower beds is the great hedge, and Sylas senses something of importance is behind it.

The night is filled with music and the scent. Kat and Tony are making out. Zoe is dancing. She stumbles and laughs at herself. David's eyes rove among the crowd. *Is he looking for Merit?* Sylas wonders, watching him. As if he can feel his eyes on him, David turns to Sylas, eyes gleaming in the firelight. "I keep waiting to wake up, you know?"

The music dissolves and some of the lights are put out, though, behind the enormous hedge is a deep, indigo glow. Murmurs ripple through the crowd. The drums start up again in a slower tempo of anticipation.

The crowd parts for a nymph with wrists tied behind his back. He struggles as two others drag him along. Vishal points and says something to Zoe and Kat, but Sylas is with David, several yards closer to the hedge, and can't make out his words. When he looks back, the prisoner has disappeared in the shadowy clusters of figures walking around the wall of the hedge where chanting begins. From behind, Viola calls, "Foundlings!" They turn to her.

She stands next to two masked nymphs. For once, she appears discomfited. "You were meant to return to the palace after the banquet. You shouldn't be here, some of the revellers got carried away, bringing you this far. Papaver will take you back to the palace now."

"What happened to that guy?" Zoe asks her.

Ignoring the question, or pretending not to hear, Viola whistles, summoning a gaggle of nymphs over. She tells them, "Go with Papaver, Solanum, and the foundlings back to the palace."

They all retreat from the glade, but Vishal lingers. Sylas, walking slowly, turns around to watch a nymph retrieve him. "Come with us!" she cries, grasping Vishal's hand. Then she laughs and licks him on the face. For an instant, Vishal appears to consider mutiny, but then, shaking his head, he allows her to lead him along with the others. As the sound of the chanting fades, Sylas hears him say, "What don't you want us to see?"

The foundlings are passive, taking in the fragrant night-blooming flowers as the nymphs guide them back to the palace. Two nymphs are holding Tony's hands. The face-licker still holds one of Vishal's, and Zoe holds his other. Sylas watches as a nymph gently grasps Kat by the elbow, whispers something to her, then guides her off the path. Sylas wants to remark upon this, to stop them, but his feet carry him onward of their own accord, and the nectar tells him not to worry about anything. Anything at all.

The palace feels newly abandoned when they arrive back. Through vined curtains, they glimpse chambers with platters of food and goblets half-full. Clothing, strewn about. In one room, an enormous basket of masks spills onto the floor.

Just as they approach their chamber, a scream pierces the night. It's from quite a distance, but full-throated and frightening in its anguish. The red-violet lights pulses in Sylas.

Everyone halts in their steps.

"What the hell!" Vishal cries.

"Oh my god, did you hear that?" Zoe looks around anxiously.

"Pay no mind, it's only mummery," a nymph titters.

"No, that sounded real—" Vishal starts to protest, but he's pressed forward by the nymphs flooding into their room as it's filled with spicy, floral smoke.

A nymph with yellow makeup like sunbursts around her eyes, holds up a pitcher of sparkling liquid. "Make merry!"

Sylas's heart is pounding in rhythm with the violet-light. He looks at David, but David is staring at the symbol again. Then a nymph appears in front of Sylas with a goblet of sparkling nectar. He drinks, and the red-violet light sputters and goes out.

5

In the soft morning light, Sylas tries to make sense of what is in front of him. Tony is lying on David's pallet along with two nymphs. Two other nymphs sleep propped up against the wall, their heads tilted together, an overturned goblet at their feet. Vishal is on his side, spooning Zoe. A nymph with damp tresses against her face spoons him.

Sylas attempts to recall the latter part of the night and comes up with only smudgy images: Tony, in a corner with two nymphs petting his face. Zoe and Vishal, entwined on the floor with a lissom nymph covered in henna. Messy hair, ripped clothes, smeared makeup. Wet, naked bodies in the pool. A lithe fellow, eyes painted like peacock feathers, sitting on the edge of the pool playing a flute. He and Sylas had had a conversation with only their eyes. Then, at some point, they'd kissed. The nectar, the Scent, the flower smoke, and the nymphs—Flute-boy in particular—had conspired to keep Sylas from worrying about David who had vanished. But not for long. Sylas had left Flute-boy to wander the halls of the palace looking for David. And that was all he recalled.

Now, Flute-boy and David are both gone. Sylas rubs his temples. His head throbs like he's wearing painfully tight goggles. He knows this headache. An ephemeral torment since childhood, made worse from the night's debauchery.

Wakefulness is catching. The nymphs yawn and stretch. The one wrapped around Vishal and Zoe lifts a languid arm and the others gently tug her to her feet. Without a word they slip from the room, one of them ruffling Sylas's hair on her way out.

Vishal is awake now and looking down at Zoe still asleep. "Last night was pretty amazing," he says softly. "If we get any consolation prize for this."

"Consolation prize for what?" Sylas asks, still rubbing his temples.

Vishal looks around the room furtively, and whispers, "I don't know. I just have a weird feeling about all of this. It doesn't—nevermind."

As if summoned from Vishal's words, the violet light flares. Sylas's heart pounds again. He looks at Tony sleeping on their friend's empty pallet. "We've lost David." He manages to say in a voice far calmer than he feels.

There is a knock on the door and Viola appears, holding a tray with two pitchers and several oblong glasses. One pitcher has water. The other contains a peridot-green liquid. "Blessed day, foundlings. I hope you slept well." She beams.

Zoe stirs and sits up.

"Thank you," says Vishal dryly. "It was quite a party."

Viola places the tray down on the table and points to the green liquid. "This will clear your mind if you indulged in too much merriment last night."

"Indulged in too much merriment," Zoe mutters and laughs darkly.

Vishal looks up at Viola with a stony expression. "More drugs, eh?"

Viola steps over to the window and draws back the curtains, dousing them in bright, scalding sunlight. "Take only the water if you prefer. When you're hungry, come to the garden. It's the first day of nusha." After a pause she adds, "you should stay in the palace today. Some of our revellers got carried away amidst the festivities." The stabbing pressure in his head makes Sylas whimper involuntarily.

When she leaves, Vishal takes the pitcher of water and pours a glass. Sylas does the same and then strips and climbs into the pool as the door opens again and David walks in, still clutching the stupid rabbit. Sylas exhales and surreptitiously swallows back tears. "Where were you?" he asks, feigning sanguinity.

David glances at Tony passed out on his bed and then flops down on Sylas's newly abandoned pallet and faces the window. His gaze drifts up to the symbol. "Just looking around," he says quietly.

Zoe presses her hands over her ears and shakes her head back and forth. "What the hell is going on?" she whispers. Vishal puts his arm back around her.

Not satisfied, Sylas asks David in a shaky voice, "Where did you go last night?"

David looks at him, eyes tranquil. "Like I said, just looking around. I wandered the palace, but I came back here after everyone was passed out." Then he says, "I don't sleep, remember?"

"Right, sorry." Sylas sighs, suppressing a pang of self-loathing. He was supposed to be supporting David, and he'd allowed himself to be swept up in last night's hedonism. "You just missed Viola," Sylas tells him quietly. "She brought us some morning medicine. I'm not sure about it, but I feel like shit."

David goes over to the table and picks up the pitcher. "Smells good."

In the corner, Tony groans. "What the—" He sits up and slowly lifts a hand to point at the symbol. "I think that was in my dream." Sylas watches as he takes in his surroundings. "Where's Kat?"

The rest of them look at one another blankly. "I don't know," says Vishal finally. "Honestly, last night's a blur." Zoe makes a little offended huff, and Vishal pecks her on the temple. "Not all of it."

"I don't think I've seen her since we were in the garden," says David.

"Yeah," Sylas agrees, he dips under the water for a moment. *And there was something else. Did he see her leave the path?* He can't tell memory from dream. He looks at David. "You didn't sleep at all?"

David shrugs. "Kinda napped on one of the hammocks outside for a bit."

Tony stands up. "Where the hell is she?" He looks out the window, squinting in the sunlight. "I don't like this." He turns to Zoe, flushes, looking guilty. "Look, I don't know if you saw me with those girls, but I swear I was out of my head. I don't know how it happened."

Zoe is quiet for a moment. Then she says, "I get it. I think we have bigger problems." She rubs her forehead. "You guys, this—this is weird."

Sylas's head is pounding. "Screw it." He leans over the pool and picks up the pitcher of green liquid and pours some into a glass. The taste is pleasantly herbal, with a hint of peppery sweetness. Tension drains from his body as he finishes the glass. A cool stream runs over his mind, soothing his pulsing brain. After a few breaths, his headache has dissolved. "It's good," he declares, looking up at them. "If you're feeling wrecked, I say go for it." The red-violet light dims and winks out.

"I don't like the color of that stuff," Vishal mutters.

David pours himself a glass and seconds after finishing, the fatigue in his face clears away and the dark circles under his eyes disappear. He hasn't looked like this in months. He smiles. "Wow."

"I'll have some," says Zoe, getting up with a grunt. "I feel worse than I did after my sister's wedding." She grabs a glass and takes a long drink, wipes her mouth with her forearm. Then she holds up the empty glass, peering at tiny dregs of nectar. "Are we prisoners?" she asks.

Sylas looks around the room. There are no bars on the window. It's a beautiful day in this beautiful place. His gaze fixes to the Symbol on the wall. He says, "There are worse places to be imprisoned."

6

They descend the curved staircase to where a few drowsy-looking nymphs loiter on the patio. The sun is high and there is a dense quality to the light that suggests it's early afternoon rather than late morning. A nymph points to a small plinth, upon which sits a bowl of round, violet-colored fruit. "For you."

There are five pieces and they each take one. The rind peels easily, revealing thick, white pith, dividing teardrop-shaped pieces of fruit. Like citrus, the rose-gold flesh is wrapped in a delicate membrane.

When the juice bursts in his palate, Sylas's heart pounds with a sparkling realization: *this* is the pinnacle of flavor—it's the most wonderful thing he's ever tasted. His eyes water. He feels light, effervescent, like he could rise into the air. His companions emit noises of pleasure. Sylas is thoroughly sated when he comes back to himself. He looks around and sees the nymphs are watching them. In their violet eyes is something like voyeurism. Sylas licks his fingers and asks them, "What is it?"

"Nusha. A gift from Nepenthe."

The foundlings are silent for a minute in the afterglow of the nusha. A breeze carries a waft of the scent from deeper in the garden. David heads toward the pleached alley and the rest of them follow. Shafts of sunlight stream through the sieve of green latticework overhead.

After a while, Sylas feels the red-violet light pricking at his euphoria. *None of this makes sense.*

Upon entrance at the garden proper. The foundlings promenade alongside endless flowerbeds, occasionally passing nymphs. They reach a field of dense moss with a single, willow-like tree next a gazebo. A dozen nymphs hold its long vines and dance around it like a maypole, while another nymph serenades from the gazebo with a chiming, percussive instrument. Kat isn't amongst the dancers.

They continue along the cobbled path and reach a crossroads going to the right and left. "Maybe we should split up," says Vishal. He's squinting, like he's trying to see beyond their immediate surroundings.

"That's not a bad idea," says Sylas.

Vishal grasps Zoe's hand. "Us three?" he asks, nodding toward Tony. He turns to David and Sylas. "You guys want to go on and we'll head this way?" He gestures with his other hand at the path on the right.

"Sure." Sylas nods, feeling a surge of gratitude towards Vishal as he realizes he hasn't been alone with David since they'd arrived at Sepal Estra.

For a little while, Sylas and David don't speak. It's the comfortable silence—even with so much to say—that he can't share with anyone else. And always, there is this ineffable thing between them. A connection or a barrier, depending on the moment. A quicksilver place that hums with shared feeling. A link as real as blood or love.

They walk along paths flanked with vibrant beds of orchids and more alien-looking blooms he doesn't recognize. They wander beneath arbors and over small bridges, crossing streams. They see squat trees that Sylas hadn't noticed before. Like Christmas trees with bowed, rounded branches, he leans down as they pass them by and sees between the leaves it's like a tent inside. Even with the subtle presence of the violet-light, a part of him wonders, *Why should we leave this place? If we find Kat, or even Merit, why shouldn't we stay? If we are allowed to.* He wants to articulate this to David, but all he can manage breaking the silence with is, "This place is amazing."

David shrugs. "Yeah." Just when Sylas thinks he won't say anything else, David adds, almost inaudibly, "dreamlike."

"Where did you go last night?"

"Just wandered."

"All night?"

David shrugs, "I told you. I napped on the hammock for a while."

Did he come back to the room while we were sleeping? Sylas wonders. *Did he see me and Flute-boy with the peacock eyes?*

When they reach the herb garden David stops to scan the handful of foraging nymphs. "You're not going to ask them if they've seen Merit?" Sylas asks after a minute.

"I don't think that's the way to go about it anymore. If she was here, they don't want me to know."

When they reach the fruit trees, Sylas stops. The fine hair on his neck stand on end as he looks around. Yesterday these trees were almost picked clean. Now they appear laden with fruit. "What is it?" David asks.

A couple of nymphs are staring at them. Remembering that they are once again thwarting Viola's instructions to stay near the palace, Sylas picks up the pace. "Nothing." They keep veering right and reach a topiary. The bushes are spheres, descending and ascending in size. Behind these is a giant hedge barricading them from going any further. They walk alongside it, moving away from the palace until an opening abruptly appears. Three paths are divided by more tall hedges going right, left, and straight ahead. "It's the labyrinth," says Sylas, recalling Viola mentioning it yesterday right before it rained.

David lights up. "I've never seen a real one like this." He strides down the center path till it's blocked and then veers left. They go one way, another. After awhile, it feels like they are doubling back, nearing and retreating from the center. Sylas wonders if David—lover of symbols and puzzles—has some method to solving this maze. Sculptures are interspersed here and there. Little knee-high nymphs with blossoms for heads. Each one a bit different.

The ever-present scent grows stronger. Time falls away. The strange circumstances fade to the background. It's just him and David and the rhythm of their steps, suspended in a dream without context. "You think Merit was here?" He glances at David.

David looks startled at the question. "I don't know," he says. "But I don't think the nymphs are honest. Or, at least they aren't telling us everything."

"Yeah, I get that feeling too." Sylas agrees.

They reach a small clearing where an enormous bush appears sculpted into the Symbol. David's eyes trace it. "What *is* it? I know there's the obvious interpretations, like it's a fertility symbol or a flower, but could it be a doorway of some sort? An entrance?"

Sylas stares at the symbol and realizes he has no sense of how much time has passed. "No one's here. We should probably be looking somewhere else." But David studies the image for another minute before moving on. They walk once more in companionable silence. Sylas unconsciously lets David get just half a pace ahead. He likes to watch him walk.

When they are down one of the narrow paths like so many others, David says quietly, "Remember that scream last night? Do you think someone died?"

"We don't really know," Sylas says. "It could have been some sort of theatre."

Pay no mind, it's only mummery.

David turns and his pale blue eyes bore into Sylas. "Do you really believe that?"

Sylas shrugs. "I guess not."

David looks back down the path, picking up the pace a little. "Thank you for coming with me. It means— Just, thank you. I don't know what's going to happen here. I'm sorry about this. I'm sorry—I think—I think we're in danger." David pauses. "And I'm sorry for hurting you."

"No, don't." *No, go on.* "Your family's been through hell."

"That's not what I mean." David's tone is different. He's staring hard at the path in front of him. His hands are fidgety. It dawns on Sylas that he recognizes these mannerisms to mean that David is nervous, hesitant.

"I'm not following."

"Never mind. I'm just sorry about before. I saw you with that nymph. And it made me think of, it made me wish—" David halts, looks around. "Wait, where are we? Didn't we pass that already?" He points to a familiar flower-headed statue.

Sylas is eager to hear what it was that David wished, but when he looks at the statue, he feels a wave of unease. An odd, outdoor claustrophobia. He has the fleeting thought that the labyrinth is made of winding entrails, consuming them. *How hard is this maze?* "I—yeah I think so. Maybe we should double back?" As they retrace their steps, he asks, "So, what were you talking about?"

David frowns and backs up, his lips moving silently as he scans the path. He's counting. "Hold on—" He jogs back to one of the crossroads and looks in either direction, brow furrowed for a moment. He says, "Let's go this way."

Sure enough, around a corner the path changes, growing wider. From behind the hedges, they hear the sound of a gong followed by cheering voices and a few seconds later, the same haunting flute song from yesterday.

They pass through a break in the hedge and are suddenly out of the labyrinth and stepping once more into a part of the garden that looks to host wildflowers. David looks relieved, but Sylas's heart sinks as he realizes the chance for them to talk is slipping away. "What were you saying earlier?" Sylas strives to sound nonchalant.

Before David can answer, a nymph makes a piercing whistle and points at them. "There they are!" she cries, as she and three others hurry up to them. The whistler looks familiar, like she might be one of the ones Tony was with last night. She lifts both forefingers and pokes Sylas and David in the chest at the same time. "*You* are wanted at the palace."

For a beat, Sylas has an instinct to resist. But he's not Vishal, to question and challenge. And David instinctively seeks the path of least resistance. They exchange uneasy glances and allow themselves to be led back down wide avenues of flower beds. It's already early evening somehow.

Through the pleached alley, nymphs pass by them, whispering to one another. Flute-boy is among them. When he sees Sylas, he winks. Sylas feels his face grow hot.

At the palace, Vishal, Zoe, and Tony sit on the lower steps of the staircase. Zoe gives a half-hearted wave and Vishal says, "No luck?"

"No." David sighs. "We found a labyrinth, but it was pretty much empty. What about you guys?"

"Lot of flowers," Vishal says irritably.

Viola strides over. She's changed since that morning and now wears a pale-yellow gossamer sarong, and thick emerald-green makeup around her eyes. "You all must stay in your rooms tonight. I could bring you more fruit or nectar if you'd like. Music and dancers, friends to make merry with."

"I just want to find Kat and get out of here," says Tony.

Zoe pinches the bridge of her nose. "Yes, some of us would like to leave now."

Viola smiles. She's looking in their general direction but not quite at them. Her gaze is just over their heads at the steps above where they are seated. "During the days of Holy Hunger, entrance or exit from Sepal Estra is forbidden."

"Forbidden by who?" snaps Tony.

Viola doesn't reply to this.

"Then I'd like to go to the ritual tonight," Vishal says.

"The ritual is not for foundlings. You will stay in the palace tonight." She glances around at the handful of other nymphs on the patio listening to this conversation. Sylas wonders if he imagines the slight appeal for assistance in her eyes.

Vishal stands up. "I'm going back to our room." He shares a meaningful look with Zoe and Tony, who follow, with Sylas and David on their heels. Viola is behind them.

When they are all inside the room, Tony closes the door, then grabs Viola. With one hand, he pins down both her arms. He whips out a knife with the other and presses it to her throat. "So now you're going to tell us what the fuck is going on."

Tension fills the room like ice water. Zoe sucks in her breath. For a moment, no one else moves. David looks dismayed, but Vishal doesn't. He's staring at Viola with a simmering rage Sylas has never seen before. As if knowing his thoughts, Vishal turns to Sylas and David saying, "I'm sorry, but we have to do something."

Tony jostles her, saying, "Where the hell is Kat?" He presses the knife to her throat harder, making an indention in her skin.

"I don't know." Viola's tone comes out higher-pitched. "Where did you get the knife?" she asks.

"Of course you'd like to know. I guess you should've kept more of an eye on us today, huh? We found a little *tool* shed? And I found an axe and since no one was around, I hid—"

"Are you going to kill her?" Zoe abruptly cuts in. "Because if you're not, you should probably shut the fuck up."

"Yeah," Vishal says. "Let's just stick to the plan here, okay?" He looks guiltily at David and Sylas. "They don't want us to see what is going to happen tonight, so that tells me it's in our best interest to know." Then Vishal opens the door. "I'll be right back," he says, and darts out of the room.

"Viola!" A nymph's voice comes up through the window from the front of the palazzo, followed by more voices and laughter. Tony yanks Viola's hair so hard that she finally makes a squeak of discomfort. He moves the knife from her throat and puts the tip against her side. "Lean over the balcony and say something that will keep them from coming up here. Understand? Tell them you're going to stay with us. Alone."

"But I'm to attend the ritual."

"Change of fucking plans then. You went last night. Ya'll take turns around here anyway, isn't that how it goes?"

Tony shuffles her over to the window. Viola calls down, "I will stay with the foundlings! Go on ahead to the ritual!" Tony pulls her back and rips part of her gown using a strip of the fabric to gag her as Vishal slips back into the room, clutching several masks and a heap of fresh petal-clothing.

Viola watches them impassively as they change. "How are you resisting it?" David asks them softly, slipping out of his clothes. Sylas steals glances at his lean, marble form. "Don't get me wrong, you're probably right to be making a bold move here, but I—I couldn't—" His gaze returns to the symbol above the window.

"I know what you mean," says Zoe, putting her hand to up David's shoulder, and looking at Vishal and Tony. "They don't feel it as much as we do."

Tony huffs. "Feel what? I was pretty fucked up last night, but that daze I felt when I first got here? Yeah, that's worn off."

"It's more than a daze," says Vishal, staring at Viola. "It's some kind of hypnosis."

Sylas struggles for a moment, then pushes through to say, "It's buried deep, but sometimes it rises to the surface." He closes his eyes. A small red-violet volcano erupts over the dark landscape of his consciousness.

It's sunset when they leave the palace. Sylas is not entirely sure what their intention is beyond finding out what happens during the ritual. "Don't draw any attention. Try not to make eye contact," says Vishal, rather unnecessarily. The mask feels like a sort of passive armor of invisibility. They try to mimic the carefree stride of the nymphs as they make their way back down the pleached alley in the growing dark. Zoe gets into character, skipping along through the garden proper. The sound of drumming accompanies their steps. David appears to be sleepwalking. The bulge in the side of his pants where he put Tucker bothers Sylas. It looks too conspicuous in his new clothes.

It's nearly dark when the murmur of the crowd intensifies and they reach the grove of giant blooms, that wonderland of inverted proportions. Sylas stares at dandelions as big as dinner plates. There are other strange flowers here: blooms like inverted starbursts that hiccup bubbles into the air, a metallic-looking lily-like flower gives off tiny sparks.

The trees are large, though not of unlikely stature. The bark glimmers an iridescent hue in the late gloaming. The violet light sputters inside of Sylas.

Nymphs are everywhere. Down on the wood floor. Up in the trees, along the bridges that, like spokes on a wheel, converge at the platform directly over something concealed behind a large hedge.

When the foundlings are offered nectar, they partake, fearing to not do so would make them stand out. The music and sound of the crowd is loud enough now to camouflage their talk. "This is where we saw that guy getting dragged off, remember?"

They start to walk alongside the hedge, as do many other nymphs going in both directions. When it breaks off abruptly, they round the corner.

And here they finally see the Goddess, Nepenthe.

The green stalk is three stories high, tapering slightly at the bottom. It changes color as it ascends. White tepals support an oblong, purple bloom the size of a giant, perpendicular bus. She radiates a muted glow like a soft lamp. The blossom *pulses*, and the sculpted, silky petals, flex. The foundlings are speechless at discovering this crowning jewel. This nexus of the mysterious power here.

"Holy shit," Vishal says finally, then he looks around anxiously. But they are not the only ones lost in awe. The nymphs dance around slowly, their violet eyes fixed to her— to Nepenthe—are brimming with worship.

Above Nepenthe, the system of rope bridges converges over a platform. Below, to the right of her, is an incongruous square structure, a shed. And surrounding her are bushes of nusha, with small, spiky purple flowers.

The music and conversation quiets as a nymph with platinum curls calls out, "Witnesses, come! Witnesses! If you watched last night, let another go ahead first! Steady, now! Remember there is a tomorrow too, and perhaps even another after that." Loose lines form by the largest trees and nymphs ascend the rope bridges. Some hang back, looking up either having already had their chance, or content to wait until another time.

"Cmon," says Tony. "This is why we came." The crowd around them converges. Nymphs laugh and jostle as they reach the ladder. Zoe and David get cut off, and surge through the crowd toward another tree. Sylas clings to Vishal's hand, grateful his friend doesn't seem to mind, as Vishal follows swiftly behind Tony to the rope ladder.

As they reach the top, the drums take on the ceremonial rhythm from the night before. When he looks down from some forty feet, Sylas is queasy. The nectar he consumed on an empty stomach doesn't help. Up here, jarring light gilds everything. He sees David and Zoe are on a bridge almost opposite them. It's soon crowded. *Please be structurally sound*, a part of Sylas thinks desperately—the part of him pulsing under a strobe of red-violet light.

The attendees shuffle toward the center, moving to the hypnotic beat of the drums. After a few more feet, they slow to a stop just as two naked figures come into view on the center platform directly over Nepenthe: Kat, and a mask-less nymph who appears to be scarcely more than a teen. His expression is somehow both anxious and stoic. The nobility stands near them: Vinca Minor, in a vermillion sarong and a crown of something like bird-bones or minced driftwood, and Helio, in a sparkling, golden chiton.

The drums cease. The crowd is quiet, waiting.

Then Vinca Minor speaks. "Blessed, Nepenthe! May your nourishment ensure ours!" She opens her arms and lowers them, palms up, beseeching, as the crowd echoes her words.

Then Helio speaks. "Flesh for fruit! Complete the circle!"

The crowd cries, ""Flesh for fruit! Complete the circle!"

Their benediction over, Vinca Minor and Helio retreat from the edge of platform. Two nymphs with spears take their place, stepping toward Kat and the young-looking nymph and prodding them toward edge of the platform.

Bile rises to his throat when Sylas understands. The red-violet let's out a scream that fades to indigo and starts to throb. "It's a pitcher plant," he blurts aloud.

"What?" Vishal looks back at him. Two nymphs pin them, eyes bright, behind their masks.

It's only a dream—this pathos and mummery. All is well among the blooms.

The nymphs murmur. Slow-dawning horror comes over Vishal's face. "Stop! Get away from there! Tony! Get her off—" his voice disappears when he's punched under the ribs.

A lanky fellow in a marigold mask hisses at him.

Sylas takes a half-hearted step forward.

"Kat!" Tony, who is ahead of Vishal, shoves his way through the crowded bridge toward her. He's almost at the platform when three nymphs accost him.

"Tony?" Kat's voice is high-pitched with panic. She looks bewildered, like she's just woken up, and flinches at the spears thrust near her face.

It happens fast amidst the shouting: the young-looking nymph next to Kat grasps her hand as his foot slips over the edge, hauling her down with him into Nepenthe. Everyone goes silent at the audible splash. A sizzling sound follows. Nepenthe expels steam as gasps echo from inside her. Then shrieking voices cry out, "IT'S! BURNING! IT'S BURN—" Shouted words melt into screams, stabbing the night air for several agonizing seconds.

When it's over, the nymphs return their focus to the imposters. Tony is red-faced, shrieking something unintelligible, his mask dangling around his neck as he writhes against his captors. Vishal is too stunned to resist as his hands are tied behind his back. Sylas doubles over, dry heaving, his whole-body slick with sweat. When he looks up, he sees Zoe, across on a bridge facing them, her hands covering her mouth. Then he finds David and struggles to make sense of what he sees. David is in a tight embrace with a nymph? In her hand is the stuffed bunny. When others pull them apart, their figures are lost in the scuffle.

For a moment it's like all the sound is off in the world. Sylas is very far from everything. And in the distance is some coming tsunami, still far off for the moment on this warm and fragrant and evil night. Then his mask is smacked off and his arms are yanked painfully behind his back, The last thing he hears is someone saying to Tony, "Shh. Shh. Don't be sad, tomorrow you will taste her in the nusha." And then something bashes into his temple, and there is only darkness.

7

The floor of the musty shed creaks as Vishal paces back and forth. It's empty, save for a small table near the door, and what Sylas assumes is a chamber pot against the far wall. David has been studying the edge of the door for what could be minutes or hours. Zoe is wedged in the corner tearing strips from the bottom of her dirty flower gown. Her hands tremble but she's stopped crying. Sylas sits in a corner opposite her with his head between his knees. He's painfully thirsty and his skull still rings. He'd been knocked out cold when they first arrived and was discomfited to find they'd all been worried for him. Another day, another headache. That green morning nectar would be heaven right now.

"So, you're saying she became a nymph?" Vishal's voice is nasally due to his broken nose.

David shrugs. "It was her."

"She had the—?" Vishal gestures to his eyes. There's a crack in one of the lenses of his glasses.

"Yeah, I think so."

"And she didn't try to help?"

David rubs his forehead. "Everything happened at once. We had just found each other. And then a second later—" He shoots a glance at Tony, who is staring at the wall, rubbing his wrists. Tony had been hog tied with firm, green vines. Vishal, David, and Zoe had removed them with some difficulty as soon as enough morning light came through the single window. The light also revealed a crude painting of the Symbol on the far wall. Whatever David was going to say, he doesn't finish.

They are all quiet for a few minutes until David says, "You alright?"

It takes a moment for Sylas to realize that David is speaking to him. He nods. "Yeah. Head hurts. I'm thirsty, but I'm alright. He closes his eyes once more.

Footsteps approach from outside. A soft knock is followed by a voice. "David? It's me, Aster." There is a pause "It's Merit. The guards said I could come in."

8

"I've heard there were a few rare births, but they happened a long time ago. Most of them just wandered in like us. Somewhere, sometime." Aster-Merit sits behind David, who's seated on the floor. He's taken his shirt off and she guides his arm out to the side so she can dab a salve onto the side of his chest. Sylas watches them until the pain in his head makes him close his eyes again.

"What do you mean? Wandered in where?" asks Vishal.

"Wandered in here—to Sepal-Estra." David lets out a little gasp and Merit tuts, "I think you've got broken ribs. Anyway, yes, so the solstices, equinoxes, maybe some eclipses—those are the times when it's possible to wander into a place like this."

Sylas envisions a celestial display of spinning planets, glinting in rhythmic sync to the light of distant stars. Then windows peering into gardens, flashing, prismatic to a time-lapse of day following night. He opens his eyes again.

"It's been happening forever. Most of us—" she pauses "—most of *them* have been here so long, their recollection of any place before is faded like the memories of early childhood."

"But where is '*here?*'" asks Vishal.

"Sepal Estra."

"Wait," David says, frowning. "The solstice came again. Why didn't you try to leave this time?"

She smiles. "Because every day is filled with merriment, and we eat the most wonderful fruit. There is no poverty or pain. No hierarchy. We take turns. Some days, I'm a dancer. Others, I pick fruit. I haven't been nobility yet, but it will be my turn soon." She finishes her ministrations and David dons his shirt. "And anyway, we *can't* leave."

"Why did you survive?" asks Zoe.

"I was supposed to be the last sacrifice, but Nepenthe only ended up taking five."

"Who were they?" asks Vishal.

"Two nymphs and three foundlings."

"From our world? Wouldn't we have heard about them?" asks Vishal. "Your disappearance was big news."

"They were from the street, I think. A man and a woman—older folks. And a guy my age, who had—I think he had mental issues. They wandered in before I did."

"But no one missed them because they were vagrants?" Zoe asks.

"I wouldn't know," Merit says, scooting over to Sylas. He sits very still as she daubs the salve on his cheek and temple, unnerved at this violet-eyed simulacrum of the girl he watched grow up. The salve smells faintly of lemongrass. Her hands are adroit and long like David's, cool against his skin. "I only saw one ritual. After it was over, Nepenthe didn't need any more. I'm not sure how they can tell this. It's some connection she has with the nobility. So I was free here. I think they like having new faces in the community."

"How do we escape?" asks Vishal.

"You can't. They will follow you. And . . ." she trails off for a moment. "There isn't anywhere to go. I tried to leave once. But I didn't get far before there was nothing in front of me. Truly, it was nothing. Not even right or left or up or down. Just fog. And I started screaming. Anything was better than that. But I guess hadn't gone too far into the nothing, fortunately. Someone found me. Grabbed my arm and pulled me back into Sepal Estra."

Zoe begins to cry again. Vishal slides down the wall next to her. "No. I don't accept this," he says.

Merit looks at them thoughtfully. "They will probably let you out today. At least within the barrier of the nusha bushes. They like for the offerings to commingle with Nepenthe before the ritual. If there was a distraction, you could try to escape and hide somewhere."

David glances in Tony's direction and lowers his voice when he asks, "Who was that guy? The other one from last night. The nymph."

"Brassicus. He looked young, but he was one of the oldest nymphs. Usually, one or two who are beloved in the community are offered. Brassicus was our sacrifice to Nepenthe. It's an honor to be part of the garden, to be nusha and feed the community." Merit leans back a little, assessing Sylas. She smiles and winks. "Any bruises under your shirt?"

"Thank you, no."

She stands. "Anyone else?"

Tony has not acknowledged her presence. He's still staring at the Symbol.

When Zoe shakes her head. Merit asks, "Vishal?"

Vishal removes his shirt revealing a large bruise under his collar bone.

"I'll do it," Zoe says, getting to her feet, and snatching the salve from Merit. "Who did they use the first night?" Zoe asks, delicately spreading the concoction onto Vishal's chest. "We saw some guy being detained. Then we heard screaming."

"Penstemon." Merit spits the word. "A troublemaker, a sadist. There are sacrifices like Brassicus and foundlings, but when Nepenthe is hungry, she is also fed those who are no great loss to the community."

After a pause, Vishal whispers, "There's got to be a way out of this. People back home will start looking for us soon. They'll find David's car just like they found yours."

How can he feel this way? Sylas wonders. How can Vishal hold onto the *before*. Sylas imagines if he was to stay another day or two, the world they'd left behind would become as insubstantial as a dream.

"It won't matter," says Merit softly, eyes turning to the symbol. "You'll never be found."

"We found you." Vishal points out.

She smiles. "True. Quite funny the garden opened up at the same place, almost the same time. They've told me it's rare, but not unheard of." She sighs. "I feel like I've been here forever."

"It's been a year," David says in a strained voice. "It's been a rough year."

Merit continues smiling, oblivious to her brother's emotions. "I'd almost forgotten you until I heard the names of the foundlings. 'David' could have been a coincidence, but then I heard 'Sylas' and 'Vishal.' I thought I'd look for you, but then I forgot again, until you found me on the bridge." Her violet eyes glow eerily in the dim light.

She forgot. Again.

"We've missed you," David says softly.

"Don't be sad for me. And don't try to leave, brother. They will kill you if you try."

"And they will kill us if we don't!" cries Vishal.

"Maybe not all of you." Merit looks around the room at each of them. "It depends on how hungry she is."

"Are there others that can go? More… criminals or whatever?" asks Sylas.

Merit shakes her head. "Not that I know of."

Sylas hesitates, then asks, "How many does she usually . . ." he trails off, unable to finish. It's too awful and absurd to ask out loud.

Merit gives a little half-shrug. "I don't know. I've heard as few as three or as many as nine."

Vishal clenches his fists and resumes his relentless pacing. His glasses are dirty. "There must be something we can do," he says. "I'm not getting eaten by a fucking plant. Is she sentient? Can we plead our case?"

The red-violet light glimmers briefly. *Oh, she's sentient, but we couldn't plead our case,* Sylas thinks. *Might as well try to plead with a flash flood or blood clot.*

"Not if she's hungry," Merit says. "Nepenthe is the reason there's a harvest every day. She is why the soil is rich and why the plants grow so marvellously." Merit's expression is rapturous. "If she were to starve, our hunger would follow, and our eyes would grow dull."

David looks at her, stricken. They are all quiet for a moment. He turns away and points to the symbol. "Do you know what that is about? I see it everywhere."

Before Merit can answer, Tony starts giggling and says to her, "What the hell are you doing here?" His eyes are glassy. He stops laughing suddenly, and gets up, snarling, "We should *kill* you."

David moves between Tony and his sister, ill-advisedly placing his hand on Tony's shoulder, he says, "I'm sorry about Kat, but this isn't Merit's fault."

"Don't fucking touch me." Tony shrugs away from him, but retreats, backs up against the wall. He's panting anxiously. "I need to get the fuck out of here."

"Hey," Zoe says gently, "We have to stick together now."

There are voices in the distance. Merit stands. "I should go."

"Wait, please, help us," says David.

They all freeze at the sound of approaching footsteps. The door opens. Viola holds a tray with nusha and nectar. She wears a scarf, but it doesn't entirely cover up the bruises on her throat. Two brawnier nymphs stand on either side of her and when she steps inside, they are right behind her.

Viola's scowls, at Merit. "Scamper, Aster."

Merit moves swiftly to vanish out the door. Once she's gone, Viola turns back to the wary figures and smiles. *She's insane,* Sylas realizes. *All of the nymphs must be.*

"Know that we are most grateful." She sets the tray down on the little table by the door.

Sylas sighs with relief. *I don't ever want to be without nectar,* he realizes. He's parched in a way he's never experienced.

Tony moves as if in a trance. He picks up a nusha and peels it with trembling hands and brings it to his mouth reverent as one taking communion. All the while staring at Viola with venom.

Sylas's mouth is watering. After Tony eats, the other three hesitantly move toward the table, their memories of the taste overpowering any possible taboo. One by one they take a piece of the fruit. It tastes even more wonderful than the day before, if such a thing is possible.

Viola says, "Glorious, yes? Your friend was nourishing."

They grunt a little at this, licking their fingers. A moment later, Tony lunges for her, but the nymphs beside her are faster and grab his arms. He hocks a wad of spit at her.

Viola flinches. A beat of fearful silence follows. She slowly wipes her face with her hand. Her eyes shine with malice. And she almost looks like she could cry. "You will be the next."

"Fuck you."

She keeps her eyes on them as she backs out the door, followed by the other two nymphs. When the door closes, Tony snatches up the tonic and begins gulping right from the pitcher, splashing some down his shirt.

"Wait!" Sylas cries. But Tony has finished almost half of it before Vishal grasps his arm, saying, "Hey, hold up— please, you gotta share. We could all use some of that." To Sylas's relief, Tony shoves the pitcher at Vishal and returns to his spot in the corner of the shed. The four of them split the rest between them. Sylas smacks his lips. The nectar has a loamier flavor than the day before. His thirst is not entirely quenched, but the pain in his head evaporates.

They are quiet for a few minutes, when David says suddenly, "They left it unlocked."

9

They emerge from the little shed next to Nepenthe, going from the sepia world inside the four walls, and into a summer day of luminous chroma. Sunlight is juxtaposed with a gossamer fog. Sylas's stomach churns with sudden queasiness and he's wobbling on a precipice over hysteria. A moment later, a pulse of ecstatic energy flows through him, quelling the nausea. He looks down at his hands. Wiggles his fingers. They are remarkable. He has no idea how long he looks at them. Time condenses, then expands. He's vaguely aware of the others.

Four nymphs surround the perimeter across the boundary of purple nusha bushes. Two of them hold sharp looking spears and watch them placidly. A waifish nymph with flaxen hair begins playing a small drum. Flute-boy accompanies her with his flute. "She likes music," explains a muscular guard with a long tawny braid, nodding toward Nepenthe. Sylas walks toward them until the guard holds out the spear. "Stay within the boundary."

Sylas backs away and turns to watch a large bubble hiccup out of the mouth of the bubble plant and drift over the nusha bushes. The image brings a profound sort of déjà vu. A bright smudge of memory that is so pure it feels like it must have been from a time not long after infancy. At the dawn of self-awareness, in some grassy park, he'd watched a bubble drift like this, a weightless, ethereal globe. The sphere had contained a secret. And now he feels that secret again, though he cannot say what it is.

When the bubble pops, Sylas's gaze falls on Nepenthe. Up close, she is majestic, monstrous. Rubbing his head, he thinks, *why am I not more distressed?* He doesn't want to be tasted by Her. He doesn't want to be tasted by everyone who eats nusha. *I would be tasted twice!* At this thought, Sylas bursts out laughing.

"What's so funny?" asks Vishal sharply, his words float out of his mouth in an orange script.

"Nothing," Sylas says, stifling more laughter. He looks around for David and sees him back by the shed.

Zoe walks a little way past Vishal and Sylas and then plops down on the grass at the edge of the boundary of purple flowers. "Come," she looks over her shoulder at them and pats the ground next to her. *"Come,"* she repeats.

"What? I'm here?" says Vishal taking a step closer to her. His words are an amber-pink now.

"No, sit next to me." Zoe leans more into her peaches-and-cream southern drawl. "Down on your fanny."

"*What* did you say?" Vishal laughs.

"Your *fan-ny.*"

They *all* laugh at that. They plop down on their fannies and laugh until their stomachs hurt.

Sylas scrunches up his face. The violet light is present but suspended somehow, static. Not pulsing, not quiet either. Brown noise. Red-violet noise. Something isn't right. Where has their urgency gone?

"You *guys.*" Zoe's voice suddenly has a note of pinkish alarm. She looks around, eyes wide and dilated.

It dawns on Sylas then and he waves his hand in front of his face and sees the tell-tale contrails.

"Oh shit," Vishal whispers. "The nectar had something different in it this time."

Vishal's words unlock something and the purple light pulses bright, loud, and throbbing before quickly being chased away by sweet scent of Nepenthe and the nusha blossoms surrounding them. The fountain burbles pleasantly and some of the falling water forms a clear, nearly camouflaged form of a small humanoid. A true sprite. He nudges Vishal to show him, but when he points, the water sprite is part of the falling water again. He takes another deep breath. He wants David. Where has he been for the last few minutes or hours? Sylas looks up from the nusha flowers to see beautiful David walking towards them, as if Sylas summoned him by thought. Sylas gets up and meets him half way.

Don't say it. Don't speak it! Sylas wills at David.

Bowling over the psychic messages, David blurts, "I think that drink was spiked."

Sylas winces and puts his index finger to his lips.

David looks around; *who isn't supposed to hear?*

It's me! I can't hear too much more. The torrent is coming. Sylas is going to cry. He wants to stay here. Everyone else is anxious to leave. Tony, Vishal, Zoe . . . but is David though? For so long all David has wanted is to find out what happened to Merit.

What is there for Sylas to go back to? He can't even recall, except for a sense of toil and technology that sapped wonder from the world. Was this so much worse? A few unfortunates to be sacrificed for the greater good? Sylas realizes that he is crying. He quickly tries to walk away. David's arms are stronger than they look when he envelops him. "Don't—don't, shhh. I'm so sorry for bringing us here." He has that faintly sweet, papery smell mixed with that fundamentally David smell that Sylas loves.

"But you didn't," says Sylas. *I'm the one who first smelled Nepenthe.* "I came with you. I want to be wherever you are." They kiss.

When he pulls out of David's arms, he wipes his face and breathes slowly, trying to calm his madly beating heart. Eyes closed, Sylas tilts his head up towards Nepenthe's blossom. After a moment, he takes David's hand and they walk back to Vishal and Zoe.

"Do you remember how she glowed last night?" asks Zoe. "You know, I've never seen a glowworm. Is that even a real thing?" She stretches out to lay on the grass on her stomach, head propped on her crossed arms.

"Bioluminescence." Sylas whispers. "The essence is illuminated." David looks serene, lost in his own world, gazing into the center of a nusha flower.

Another nymph comes through the arbor. Vishal stands up and starts laughing. There's no color to his voice now, but the sound is a staccato trail, and the trail is leading them into the future and closer to their unfortunate fate.

Sylas puts his hands over his ears, but when he does this, the red-violet light blasts inside of him. He wants to crawl out of his skin. He must hide, hide, *hide*! After all, he is a street person like those she had instead of Merit. Or he perhaps might have been if it wasn't for the Fairchilds. Where can he hide? Inside the palace? Inside a closet? A cupboard. Would he fit? Proportions are strange in Sepal Estra. Could he burrow in the earth like a worm? *A glow worm!* This thought triggers laughter again.

Zoe laughs again too, and her laughter joins Vishal's. Hers is lighter, sparkling, dancing steps trailing around his. Sylas watches Zoe and Vishal and he finally sees how strong of a bond they've formed in this short time. He wants to hug them both.

Zoe catches her breath, says, "Oh man, oh my god." Then her face falls. Sylas follows her gaze over to Tony who is stumbling around Nepenthe, talking to himself. Zoe bites at her fingernails and speaks quickly. "I've known Kat since 6th grade. We went to her sister's baby shower last week." She drops her voice to a conspiratorial whisper, "I don't like him right now." She points to Tony. "Honestly, I've never liked him." She suppresses a giggle. "He's a neanderthal. I never told her though. I never told her how I really felt about him."

David, Vishal, and Sylas are silent at this admission. No one wants to talk about Tony. Or be near him. He's *next*, after all.

Sylas scoots away from the nusha bushes to sit nearer to the fountain flanked by a pair of strange willows. The grass here is so thin and soft it's like sitting on a carpet of emerald eyelashes. He catches a glimpse of little drops of water against the stone. The droplets are rainbow spheres. He remembers that he'd almost remembered something about droplets. No, it was rainbows. No, it was bubbles. He shakes his head and turns to David. David stares at the burbling fountain, a faint smile on his face. *Does he see the water sprite?* He scoots closer to Sylas and rests his head on his shoulder. And Sylas feels he's never been in a more perfect place. A more perfect moment. Circumstances aside.

Vishal sits next to Zoe who is twirling a flower. "How did this happen?" he asks.

"Well," Sylas clears his throat. "Obviously they spiked the nectar or whatever." He looks up and the cornflower blue sky appears to be layered with faint, moving fingerprints.

"That's not what I mean. Is this an alternate dimension?"

"Maybe it's another planet," Zoe whispers.

Their voices fade in and out as waves of anxiety and euphoria chase one another.

Sylas looks at Nepenthe and recalls the terrible sounds Kat and Brassicus made. He imagines what he hasn't let himself imagine up to this point: their skin melting from their faces until, for an instant, it's just their skulls, screaming. Sylas squeezes his eyes shut and shakes his head, trying to lose the thought and fling off the encroaching panic.

After a few deep breaths, he blinks and takes in their surroundings once more. Tony has moved away from Nepenthe and is staring madly into the face of the auburn-haired nymph, who seems game for a staring contest. With growing unease, Sylas recalls Tony drank more of the nectar than anyone else.

Nepenthe pulses and glows. The spell breaks and they look at one another, fearfully.

Vishal stands up saying, "I'm not dying this way. I'm going to talk to her." Sylas watches as Vishal walks over to Nepenthe and circles underneath her great stem, speaking quietly before sitting down crossed legged at her base, his posture neat as a fencepost. He presses his palms together and bows his head like a yogi.

Tony says something incomprehensible to Auburn hair, then storms off toward the rest of them. Drummer girl and Flute-boy carry on with their music.

As Tony approaches them, they move away, getting up to join Vishal and sit near Nepenthe.

Sylas observes his friends. Zoe seems like a punky urchin. With his shaggy blond hair and pale, pre-Raphaelite face, David is a glamorously consumptive poet from a period piece. Vishal, with his broken nose and glasses, is a refugee from a war-torn city.

Soon, despite his earlier violent laughter, Vishal becomes a soothing presence. The drug has peaks and valleys, Sylas is realizing. He runs his hands through the eyelash grass and euphoria dissolves the delineation between him and his surroundings. He's part of the sky, the plants, the soil. He closes his eyes and he's part of *Her*. His flesh is plant matter. His bones are soft stone. His sweat is nectar, his blood, sap.

Sylas lifts his head. In the expanse above, he sees visions of endless gardens, overlayed by faded time-lapse glimpses of buds opening. Plant vulvas and birthing seeds exploding into profusions of flowers. The Symbol appears and disappears in the glorious kaleidoscopic bouquets. The images move to the music of flute and drums.

"Are you asking her? Praying to her?" Zoe whispers to Vishal. Sylas looks at him and sees Vishal frowning in concentration.

Tony is over by the fountain now. His voice carries, but his words are incomprehensible. He punches the air, as if scrapping with an invisible foe, then groans, shoving all his weight against the fountain. Sylas recalls that he once heard hallucinogens could sometime precipitate schizophrenia in individuals who are predisposed to the illness. *Don't think about that. Don't think about Tony.*

Vishal opens his eyes suddenly and says, "Maybe someone should create a diversion so the rest can escape, and—"

There's a loud thud, followed by a strenuous groan. Tony has knocked the fountain off its base, and with unfathomable strength, he picks it up and plunges through the nusha bushes, parting the two guards, smacking the auburn haired one on the temple, who falls limp to the ground. Then Tony drops the fountain, runs through the arbor and out into the garden.

Escaped. Just like that.

The drummer nymph falls to her knees, shrieking over the felled guard. The other rushes off to pursue Tony while Flute-Boy changes his tune to something faster and urgent. This strikes Sylas as hilarious, and he starts giggling again. Standing, the drummer girl turns a furious gaze at them.

They scramble to their feet. Vishal holds his hands up. "We didn't know he was going to do that!"

Zoe smacks his shoulder. "Don't *apologize* to her."

"I didn't—"

"We should run now," says Sylas. But when he looks at his three remaining companions, they are glassy-eyed, maladroit as zombies. And he knows he's the same.

They all turn again at the sound of shouting and thundering footsteps followed by an almost inhuman roar. Tony runs back through the arbor, an axe raised over his head. Drummer girl attempts to intercept him, and Tony brings the axe down, splitting her small skull open like a melon.

Zoe screams.

Tony yanks the gory axe out of the nymph's head, and continues running, back through the nusha bushes and towards them.

Vishal, Zoe, David, and Sylas all dart out of his way, but they aren't his target.

When the axe hits Nepenthe's stem with a wet thwack, Sylas winces. Nepenthe's bulb pulses a radiant indigo light.

More nymphs rush through the arbor and barrel past them; one knocks David to the ground. When Sylas holds out his hand, David looks up at him uneasily for a moment before taking it. "What?" Sylas asks.

"Your eyes," David whispers, then retches.

Sylas blinks and looks around. The nymphs are flooding across the barrier, crying and gesticulating.

Vishal surreptitiously edges closer to the boundary.

"Don't move!" cries a freckled, androgynous-looking nymph, with an upside-down flower for a cap.

When Sylas looks back, he sees the axe has been wrested away from Tony who's been tackled to the ground. Papaver heaves the axe up, and brings it down on Tony's right arm, cleaving through flesh and bone. Then he drops the axe, picks up the severed arm, and slaps Tony in the face with his own hand as another nymph picks up the axe and lops off Tony's left arm.

Flute boy continues to serenade everything with his macabre tooting.

As blood pools swiftly around Tony, Vinca Minor strides up commanding, "Stop! Do not waste him." Her white gown is splattered with blood. Behind her, a nymph rushes forward clutching a bundle of the same vines Tony had been contained with inside the shed. Tony's eyes are dull as tourniquets are quickly placed around his gushing stumps. His skin is alabaster. Then he's hauled to his feet, dragged to the foot of a nearby tree, swiftly secured in a harness, and cinched up to the rope bridges.

Nymphs hover around Nepenthe, murmuring, stroking her, one of them applying to the exposed tissue what looks and smells like the same salve Merit tended to them with. The wound isn't severe in the context of Her size and Sylas feels relieved at this. *Why?* he wonders.

Another drummer starts a familiar tempo, and Flute-Boy modifies his tune to accompany her in a version of the previous evening's ritual music. Next to him, David makes a sort of whimpering sound. It's early for the ceremony, but under the circumstances it does not seem to matter. The two felled nymphs are solemnly wrapped in violet sheets as others begin to chant.

Above, two guards drag Tony to the center platform. His arms make plopping sounds as they are flung down into Nepenthe. He wears a vacant smile as he's goaded off the end. Sylas cringes at the splash. Nepenthe starts to hiss and steam.

"Run!" Vishal cries. Sylas shakes off the enchantment and turns to see Vishal has kicked the guard and taken his spear. "Run!" he cries, again. "Run, now!"

Sylas looks around for David. He's gone. Then Sylas glimpses him far ahead, already through the arbor, running alongside Merit. Somehow they've covered a lot of distance.

Sylas bolts, running behind Vishal and Zoe with the adrenalin of the condemned. He tears through the arbor and when a nymph blocks his way, he shoves her aside. Vishal calls over his shoulder, "To the woods!" Sylas follows. *David, hide. Be safe.*

Ahead, more nymphs appear on the sides of the path and he veers off of it, plunging through bushes where thorns scratch him. He barrels on, until he stumbles into an open space—the topiary. Then it's just a short distance to the squat trees with the drooping branches that form little tents nestled on the wood floor. He goes under one and curls into a tight ball and closes his eyes. *If I can't see them, they can't see me.*

There are footfalls. Calls in the distance. Long spells of silence. Adrenalin slowly siphons away. Sylas's psyche burrows down a deep hole inside of himself, to a place of dreams, if not quite sleep. An intermission, where he wanders in his mind's eye. He roams in a garden of violet flowers, and thorns popping bubbles. And beneath it all, he clings to his dear hope. His fantasy: *maybe we will both live. No more worries about what happens after school is over. This place is an equalizer. No perpetual obligation to feel grateful. Of having to always feel like I'm just not quite one of them. Not knowing if David loves me. Loves me like that. Because he does!*

Sylas plays a reel of pleasant fantasy. He and David live in the garden. David walks amidst the fruit trees under a beam of sunlight. The two of them forever lounging by the pools and laughing and picking fruit thrusting themselves into each other.

And if we don't live, if Vishal or Zoe or both are the ones to escape? Well, perhaps there are worse fates than being joined in an enormous flower like some reverse twin birth and then composted into a beautiful garden. Merit must have pulled David aside. She must know of a place for him to hide… A voice whispers, *"Why didn't they get you? Did David even try to help you?"* They must have. David must have called to him, and Merit must have urged David along, pulled him along. Maybe he thought Sylas was right behind them. Yes. That is what it must be. Because they were one. He doesn't think about the way David had looked at him. "Your eyes," he'd said.

And what if it comes down to the two of us? Sylas is trying to be quiet beneath the shielding branches, but at this thought he can't help but let out a whimper.

Which of us is more deserving? He suspects the scales tip in David's favor. David was devoid of darkness. Sylas remembers how David wrapped his arms around him earlier. And David would be with his sister. Sylas stifles a sob when the answer comes to him: *be the rescuer, not the rescued. It must be me to go into Nepenthe.* Gritting his teeth, Sylas vows: "I will be his nusha." He gasps, nauseated with fear but a part of him is at peace. Then the red-violet light bursts, melting into glittering streaks, smeared purple stars.

10

"There! There!" The voices of the nymphs pierce his dreams sometime later. "Clever foundling!" Sylas's back scrapes along the ground as he's dragged out from beneath the tree's protective branches. He's hauled to his feet and the nymphs guide him back toward the heart of the garden. He doesn't attempt to bolt. At this point, defiance will only cause more physical pain. "You silly thing," says Solanum. Sylas somehow recalls her name from that first night. She'd been one of Tony's distractions. "*All* of you silly things! We got you all, you know."

Of course they had. The nymphs were on the hunt, fearful of not finding their sacrifices in time. Not wanting to be nusha themselves.

It's just past sunset. Sylas has come down from the drug trip, and now his heart is pounding with both relief and sober dread. He keeps his eyes on the path as, sooner than seems possible, he's marched past the topiary and reaches the enormous blooms that herald the nusha bushes and Nepenthe. He doesn't forget his promise to himself. *Be the rescuer. If I can save David, I will.* But how he wants to stay in this garden and drink the nectar and live forever. Or at least for a long, long time. *I don't want to die. I don't want to be nusha. Not yet.*

His eyes sting with tears as he hears piteous weeping and sees Zoe. Sobbing, she's being marched on, hands tied together in front of her. Her shoulder is covered in blood that drips down her ragged petal gown. Ahead of her are two nymphs, each hauling a rope tied to the wrists of a limp, bloody figure. Arrows puncture Vishal's throat and chest. Sylas's legs are about to give out. He releases an involuntary cry. Vishal's image blears with Sylas's tears. *It's better for him—* Sylas thinks. *He didn't want to be Nepenthe's meal.*

Zoe's face is dirty and wet, when she sees Sylas, she gulps between sobs, "We got to the forest again. We got pretty far. The world looked different. Like before. Like home, but—"

The beat of the ritual music begins.

Sylas blinks away tears and scans the faces around him for David and finds him next to Merit, eyes bloodshot, staring, stricken, at Vishal.

David, Sylas, and Zoe are shepherded to the base of a tree where a ladder leads up to the rope bridges. One by one they ascend.

The drums go quiet. Viola, the nobility, and a cluster of other nymphs stand on the platform over Nepenthe. Vinca Minor looks impassive. Helio, mildly irritated as if he's ready for this holiday to be over.

"A waste," Viola says looking over the bridge and down at Vishal. She's changed clothing since she visited the shed this afternoon and now she wears a blood-red gown. "Two of you could have stayed. Even with all the trouble you've wrought. Now, two of you must feed Nepenthe."

Viola looks between the three of them for a moment, then she tosses her chin at Zoe. "Her."

Zoe kicks and screams as two nymphs strip off her dress and drag her to the platform. The drums resume, this time with chanting, but the sacred words are difficult to hear against Zoe's cries as she's thrown into Nepenthe.

Let it be over with. Sylas clenches his fists enduring Zoe's screams for several torturous seconds. He looks at David, trembling and pale.

Viola raises her voice and addresses the nymphs surrounding them with spears. "Bring them over. They can decide for themselves." She looks at them and smiles.

After they are quickly stripped, David walks slightly ahead of Sylas as they are nudged onward. When they reach the platform, David peers down over the edge. Sylas takes a step closer, "David, don't." He grows almost calm, resigned. His eyes brim with tears. *It will hurt, but not for long, and then he will love you even more when he tastes tomorrow's nusha.*

David lets out a dark little chuckle. "Check it out." His voice sounds strange. "At least we get the answer to one question," David beckons Sylas closer.

"What is it?"

"You can see it if you look from here."

Sylas's heart hammers faster. He recalls David and Merit running away amidst the chaos wrought by Tony. They had not looked back. David had not looked back. Like there was nothing between them. No blood, no love. He sees David returning the morning after the first night here.

"Where did you go?"

"You know I don't sleep."

Did David already know Merit was here then? Had he already found her? And now David is looking at him and is there a twinkle of *amusement* in his eyes? Could it be deceit? "Come," Did he just bend his knees a sliver, jouncing the platform?

Poisonous anguish floods Sylas's whole body. Dismay so powerful it hits like a punch to the gut. *What is this? No, David. I'm only rescuing you if you're better than I am. And how can you be the better one if I'm willing sacrifice myself for you?*

It's an impulsive, lizard-brained decision. A quick little shove is all it takes. There is a fleeting look of bewilderment on David's beautiful face as he teeters. He lets out a gasp of surprise.

Sylas turns away, covering his ears to drown out the obscene sounds of David being digested inside of the flower goddess. As he walks back, faces—luminous in the torchlight—observe him. More of the nymphs have come up onto the bridges. Flute-boy and Merit among them. Tucker dangles from where she clutches it by an ear. Her expression betrays nothing, but a single tear slips from her eye and runs down her cheek. The drums slowly taper to a soft pulse. There is a tacit understanding that Nepenthe will not sigh again until the next time the stars align.

Sylas reaches the platform where Viola and the nobility stand, appraising him with interest. *Didn't expect me to be the last one, did you?*

Helio descends the ladder, followed by Vinca Minor. Viola lifts out a hand to Sylas, but he freezes a few feet from her. That light of panic that started red and turned violet and then indigo is now a cold shade of the palest blue. He turns around, moving quickly back toward Nepenthe. Viola calls his name softly.

Heart pounding, Sylas reaches the platform. There is no sign of David, but from this view, looking down into Nepenthe, Sylas sees the Symbol. It emerges in the layered curves of her petals. All those renderings of it in the palace and garden and here it is. The true form. *"At least we get one of our questions answered."* Sickness and regret surge through Sylas and he falls to his knees and drops his face into hands, keening.

Behind him, Viola calls, "Come back, dear one. Tomorrow, you will taste him in the nusha!"

And later that night, having spent his tears, Sylas is plied with nectar. He partakes and makes merry. The next day, his heart is further healed, and his eyes glow vivid purple when he tastes David and the others in the nusha. And after a time Sylas is called by the name Rhylid. Rhylid spends his days with Flute-boy, whose name is Ruel, and Aster and others. All of his new brothers and sisters. Some mornings, ardent, and high on nectar they prostrate themselves before their beloved Nepenthe, without whom they would vanish. And between Sylas and Nepenthe flickers an amethyst communion of light between this mother and her child. And when he feels her blessing, he gets to his feet, bows his head to her, and runs off to frolic as her fortunate children are meant to do.